BIG
GIRL

STORIES FOR
THE REST OF US

BIG GIRL

STORIES FOR THE REST OF US

HOWARD LUXENBERG

Stories from this collection have appeared in slightly altered form in
the following publications: "The Photograph" in *Tin House* and *Best
of Tin House*; "Getel" in *The Iowa Review*, "The Stove" in *The Sun;*
"Tag Sale" in *The Gettysburg Review*; "Civics Lesson" and "Lake
Moriah" in *Alaska Quarterly Review;* and "The Hill" in *Other Voices.*

Big Girl / Howard Luxenberg. – 1st ed.
ISBN 978-0-578-51350-8

For Paula

Contents

Big Girl   1
The Photograph   13
Tag Sale   35
The Stove   61
Civics Lesson   71
The Hill   87
Lake Moriah   101
Getel   111

About the Author   117

Big Girl

She was the most beautiful girl in our high school, and no one asked her out. She had a mane of reddish gold hair and green eyes. She had a big smile full of straight white teeth. She was tan, just back from summer vacation. She was perfectly proportioned. She was 6 feet, 10 inches tall.

She was the biggest girl – the biggest person – any of us had ever seen. She towered over our basketball players.

She was graceful, although to be honest her grace was constrained a little by the need to not trample us underfoot. She needn't have worried; people tended to get out of her way.

She had none of the awkwardness that afflicts tall people; she made none of their stooping concessions, their physical apologies for being too tall. She walked down the hall with her head high, her shoulders back, her diminutive notebook clutched to her ample breasts, her wide smile, her big green eyes.

She disgusted people. It's incredible, but she disgusted people. She was just so damn big and so damn beautiful and it made people's skin crawl to see such beauty *wasted* on such a monstrously large canvas.

People would look at her and feel uncomfortable. She was not just beautiful, she was extraordinarily beautiful. And that would have been enough right there to make people uncomfortable. She was not just big, she was extraordinarily big, and that made people uncomfortable. And the combination of too big and too beautiful worked some strange math of its own, so that she created an exponential discomfort around her. People could not help but look at her; could not stop looking at her, could not help but be disgusted as they looked at her. It was the damnedest thing.

Her name was Sassy. It was a peculiar name. People would get it wrong and call her Suzie, or Sally, or Sissie.

How big was she? She filled a doorway, had to cock her head slightly as she entered. A normal person's straight ahead gaze would catch square in the tits. She wore mostly men's clothes, from the Big and Tall shop.

How big was she? Seated, she was taller than most of the freshmen. She could reach the map in Social Studies without using the hooked end of the pointer.

How big was she? Big enough to palm a basketball. Big enough that *Gulliver's Travels* was discreetly dropped from the curriculum. Too big and too beautiful to fit with any notion, any adolescent notion, of how the world should be.

We were often thrown together, in this, our senior year. I was the shortest boy in the class. I wasn't a midget, or a dwarf, or some case of arrested development, I was merely, and as luck would have it, a quarter inch shorter than Preston Fillbert. Of course, Ken, the yearbook editor and reigning asshole, decided we should be Class Couple, Sassy and I. There were genuine class couples, pairs that had been together since Junior High. There were three such couples, and the truth was Ken didn't have the courage to choose from among them. So he chose Sassy and me, unable to resist the photographer's dream our juxtaposition would make.

I was thrilled. My crush on Sassy was bigger than she was. I could imagine that she was not thrilled. I was short, but I was not a freak. I was short, but I might still grow some. And there were girls, enough, about my height. Sassy was good-natured about it in front of me. But I heard that she called Ken an asshole when he first brought the idea up.

At the photo shoot our pose was modeled on the famous credit card ad that featured Wilt Chamberlain and Willie Shoemaker, the jockey. We stood back to back, our arms crossed, our sides to the camera. Ken wanted us to scowl – Class couple, get it? – but I was too pleased to have my back pressed up against Sassy's, to do anything but grin. Sassy, in spite of the humiliating circumstances, was smiling too. Ken finally gave up and took the picture.

Afterwards, Sassy apologized to me.

"Why?" I asked.

"Because if it wasn't for me, no one would take any notice of your being short."

"That's not your fault."

Sassy was silent, her thoughts having moved on to other matters. I wasn't ready to give up the conversation. "It's not your fault Ken's such a prick."

"He is, isn't he?"

I was small, but I had earned a grudging respect as a wrestler. I wrestled at 102, which meant, small as I was, I had to lose a few pounds before each meet to make weight. So I put on my rubberized sweat suit and trotted around the gym until I was as wet with my own sweat as if I had showered in it.

The cruelest, because it was the cleverest, dig at Sassy was a cartoon that Schultzie drew. Schultzie was way beyond talented, so much so that we all were certain he would be famous one day. He had a particularly vicious way of depicting us – giraffe-like necks; weak, Norman Rockwell chins; Dumbo ears; Adam's apples the size of goiters – and in this particular picture, two such teenage monstrosities were holding what was clearly a girlie magazine, ogling the foldout. But the foldout had more than three panels; it had about ten. The back of the foldout was what we saw, the ogling boys face us, and a helpful arrow led from the foldout to the caption balloon: "You know who."

Schultzie was a quiet, introverted kid, who spent all his time cartooning. In each class he sat and drew his version of what was going on, our brief chronicler. It seems remarkable to me now that no teacher ever interfered with this. I can only guess that they recognized his genius, and wisely and uncharacteristically let him pursue it. His real name was Brian Washington, but everyone called him Schultzie. He was a slight black kid, the color of India ink, and so black his close-cropped hair seemed gray in comparison. "That's pretty mean," I told him when I saw his foldout cartoon of Sassy.

"I draw 'em as I see 'em." It wasn't a defiant statement. He said it almost apologetically. He seemed to mean he had no choice.

In English class he drew the balcony scene from Romeo and Juliet. Juliet/Sassy stands on the ground but reaches up and through the balcony with her head and shoulders. A diminutive Romeo flaps his arms to hover a couple of inches above the ground and speaks his famous lines in a balloon: "What light . . ." Romeo bears an unmistakable resemblance to me. I colored when Schultzie showed it to me.

"You dig her, don't you?" he said.

I didn't deny it.

* * *

5

The guy from Playboy turned out to be a woman. She arrived in a limo, for Chrissake. She was pretty, and well dressed in a businesslike way. It made you think she was a former playmate herself, and I suppose that was the idea. Schultzie heard about it and went right to work. He had to undulate the limo to make it fit on the page, so the effect was snakelike, a cobra coiled back on itself, its hood, the limo's hood rearing up, ready to strike Sassy. Sassy, her back to us, had pulled her blouse open and was flashing the snake-limo.

Those of us who were obsessed with Sassy – me, Schultzie, a couple of our friends – hung out near her house when she told us about the interview. ("Interview?" Schultzie asked. "Interview? What, your tits got something to say to this woman?") We thought we were going to see Hugh Hefner himself, but we were happier to see this ex-playmate business-woman. The woman invited Sassy into the limo and they drove off. They drove off to the Playboy building downtown, where they went about impressing the living shit out of Sassy. (Of course she impressed the living shit out of them, too.) I tried to imagine it, and even after Sassy described it, in all its sumptuousness, the incredible furniture, the incredible carpets, the incredible art on the walls, I couldn't see it in my mind's eye. Schultzie drew a pack of bunnies offering an enthroned Sassy a glass slipper. The slipper was the size of a small boat.

"You gonna do it?" I don't remember who said this. We all had the same question so it didn't really matter who uttered it. We felt proprietary toward Sassy, and we expected to be consulted about this decision, as if the body in question were ours. Sassy played it coy, and couldn't be coaxed into answering. I think she liked the attention – well maybe that's not quite right, she always got plenty of attention – but she liked the particular tenor of this attention. The Playboy folks were good at giving the right kind of attention.

While Sassy was busy being coy, we were doing our research. Schultzie had several years' worth of Playboys, and we were up in his room looking through them, trying to extrapolate from past issues the extent to which this would humiliate or legitimize Sassy. We were calibrating the tastefulness of these spreads: how would we feel if they made Sassy pose like *that*. The centerfolds were okay: they had a light chirpy quality, the girls looking like they were surprised, but happy to be caught without their clothes on. They weren't sleazy or provocative. Some were silly; usually these were ones with a phony coyness, and we resolved to warn Sassy away from poses like those. I was looking for something else. Were there props that gave away, or, worse, called attention to the girls' size? One particularly short girl was posed next to a bar stool, which made it clear she was no giant. How would they choose to show off Sassy's height? Schultzie looked for a while with us; but later, when I came up for air, I saw he was drawing.

Schultzie's room was a corner room with paned windows on two sides. Light, filtered by a leafy maple tree floated in. The room contained a simple desk, a hardbacked chair, chest of drawers, bed – all old furniture that looked like it belonged to my grandparents' generation. Remarkably, the walls were bare; but I could see his sketchbooks lined up in a small bookcase. There must have been fifty of them; they looked like a set of encyclopedias. In Schultzie's cartoon, the windows were small and high and let in a feeble light. We were dressed like explorers in pith helmets and safari jackets, we were poring quizzically over papyrus scrolls. On a throne, a statue of a black prince, in royal Egyptian regalia, holding a hooked staff looks out from the picture with one unseeing eye, and sardonically down at the explorers with the other.

"We can't let her do it." I said. "They'll make big deal out of her height."

No one agreed with me. They insisted that the spreads were, all in all, tastefully done. Clearly they were looking forward to autographed copies and whatever deflected glory would come their way from knowing her.

I needed a break from all those unavailable centerfolds. I took down one of Schultzie's sketchbooks.

"Put it back." Schultzie's voice was a quiet command. I started to respect it, but Lipsy who was with us, grabbed it from my hand.

"Let's see some of the old stuff."

"Put it back." Same tone.

"Take it easy. We won't rip it or anything."

"Put it back, asshole." No longer a quiet command. There was heat and even something pleading beneath it.

Lipsy must have heard it too, because he suddenly became more interested in it. "What's in here?" Lipsy's voice smirked.

"It's personal. Put it back." Schultzie lunged at Lipsy, but Lipsy screened him with his back. Schultzie pinned Lipsy's arms to his side and he dropped the book.

I wanted to respect Schultzie's wish but my curiosity got the better of me. Besides, Lipsy was more my friend than Schultzie was. I picked up the sketchbook and opened it. There was a sketch of Sassy, naked, bound by a thousand threads, surrounded by Lilliputians, tiny versions of ourselves.

"You fucking assholes. You fucking assholes." Schultzie said it over and over again, a sound like keening at a wake. I turned the page, the pages; all sketches of Sassy, most naked.

"Has Sassy seen these?" Lipsy sounded indignant, which I thought was out of place. I told him to shut up. It seemed to me later that at that moment each of us was alone with thoughts that made us uncomfortable. I kept turning the pages. Lipsy kept looking. Schultzie puttered around his own room like a

9

stranger, putting away the Playboys, muttering "fucking assholes, leave already" over and over until we finally did.

★   ★   ★

Sassy's Day of Decision was Friday, October 31st. Halloween. Schultzie managed a lame (for him) cartoon of Sassy split down the middle, half fig leaf, half nun's habit. The trees were bare; the leaves a brown slush underfoot. A heavy sky, gray, metallic weighed down on us. It was cold, it was raw, you could see each breath. It was hard to imagine anyone naked.

But all the students at N____ High School could think of nothing else. Even Halloween paled before Sassy's imminent decision, one that would catapult her into the flesh hall of fame, or leave her with us in obscurity. Schultzie, whose job it was to chronicle the elusive daily aura of our school, wasn't up to the task. Normally so still, he was agitated, wound up. He drew that one lame picture of the divided Sassy, but what we wanted from him was some picture of how we felt: our doubts, our anticipation, our profound agitation. "The school feels like one big hard-on," Schultzie said, but he didn't draw anything. That probably covered it for the boys. But what about the girls? What had turned up their voltage?

There was the money, of course. The $25,000 payment for posing was almost as much as the teachers made in a year. It would pay for a year at college

– a couple of them. It would buy a car. It would take the rest of us 4,000 hours of dunking French fries in boiling oil at minimum wage to earn that. But would we sell our souls for $25,000?

That was the point of an editorial in the school paper. Like most school paper editorials, it made me want to puke. First off, its author was dying to see Sassy naked. Secondly, as far as I could tell, people routinely sold their souls for a lot less. Just walking into school we sold our souls, or at last discounted them. We all did; all except Schultzie. Schultzie honored his soul. He drew, and nothing else. Even in gym, if he didn't feel like whatever game we were playing, he drew. The rest of us gave ourselves away little by little to things we hated: French, Chemistry, Algebra, Western Civ.

"What's the good word, Sassy?" Ken called to her.

"Go fuck yourself, Kenny," Sassy replied, but without much venom.

"My, we're edgy today." Ken didn't give up easily, and he always took the last word.

Sassy made her way to her locker. She squatted before the combination lock, twirled it and banged it open. She deposited her parka and scarf inside. She took a deep breath, but she banged it shut anyway. The bell rang.

Among the boys, the rumor was she would say "yes." Among the girls, the rumor was she would say "no."

At 2:40, the bell rang and the school exhaled its students. The black limo was parked outside. We gasped when Hugh Hefner himself got out.

Of course, it was Schultzie that he came for in the black limo. If you've read any O. Henry, you could have seen that coming a mile away. Sassy had shown him Schultzie's work, that's how we figured it. And it made a great headline: Young Black Cartoonist From Ghetto Breaks Into Playboy. Of course Schultzie wasn't from the ghetto, but he was young enough and black enough. He was a little light on attitude for this particular fairy tale, but they would work with him on that. There was still the business of Sassy's nude poses for Schultzie; we could never get our minds around that, so we just dropped it after a while. I grew a few more inches and a few more pounds and gave up wrestling and freakishness. Rumor had Sassy all over the place: in the Netherlands, where big people are the norm; in a strip joint out by the airport; cloistered in a nunnery in New Mexico; transported to wherever people needed her to be to ease their own discomfort. For myself, I never could decide where she went.

The Photograph

It is a strange feeling to see yourself paired in a photograph with the deceased. The dead man is my late uncle Jake. In the photo we are on the broad green lawn, by the arboretum, a trellis of wild roses serving as backdrop. I am in a tux with hounds tooth tie and cummerbund; Uncle Jake is in a pale blue evening gown; a Dior, I believe. He has an arm draped over my shoulder in avuncular bonhomie. We are holding cigars and staring at the camera, mugging for it. One thin dark shadow creeps across the lawn at our feet. From the flagpole, I would guess. It's late afternoon in the photograph.

I can see the spot now, through the library windows. It's pretty much the same. The grass and the roses are paler in the sharp light of noon. The library is the only two-storied room in the house, so I'm sitting in the leather wing chair to compensate, I guess, for the vastness of this internal space. I like the library, but only if I'm in this chair. This is the room that most impresses guests. "I would kill for this room," a literary friend of Father's confessed once, and promptly fell into a thoughtful silence in which, I swear, she was working out exactly whom she would have to kill for this room to become hers. The wall facing the arboretum is mostly windows, twenty feet tall and paned. The three remaining walls are books, each tunneled by a door, and, in one case a fireplace. (We once played Cask of Amontillado in that fireplace; I stood inside it while my brothers bricked me in with books until my screams brought Mother.)

You'll want to know about Jake's evening gown and his death. I'll get to that. Right now I want to tell you, selfishly, about how I feel seeing myself in this photograph. Strange is too vague. I feel out of place, like I had worn the wrong clothes to a party. Dressed up, when everyone else was casual. Or maybe the reverse: I imagine death is a more formal place than this. Still, that's not quite it. The picture looks to me like one of those marvels of modern special effects, where some of the characters are live actors, and some are cartoons. I am the live actor, Jake is the cartoon. We're from two different worlds now. I can't quite explain it. Go find a picture of yourself with someone you love who's dead. You'll see what I mean.

Jake is the youngest of my father's three brothers. In the picture, he is in his forties. He is wealthy, like my parents, like all his brothers. Balzac said that behind every great fortune is a crime. The crime behind ours is the Civil War. The Blue and the Gray:

we outfitted the Blue. Millions of shoddy, over-priced uniforms that lasted barely long enough for their owners to die in. Afterward we could afford to make better uniforms and price them fairly. We diversified into commercial uniforms: the grease monkey under your car is probably wearing one of our coveralls. That's all sold now, and invested. We live off the return.

★   ★   ★

Mother took Jake's death stoically, but hard. "He was like a sister to me," she admitted in an unguarded moment. Mother was a middle child, sandwiched between two boys. When she left home to marry Father she exchanged one barracks for another. Then she bore four boys, so that all her living relations were male. It must have been lonely for her, I realize now.

She so forgot herself with Jake that she had had a long confiding chat with him about her menopause. "I'm fine one moment, and the next I'm basting in my own juices."

"Yes. It's hell on silk. It's never quite right after you've sweated it. They're old fashioned, but have you tried arm guards?"

★   ★   ★

"I want a girl." Mother expressed her desires in simple imperative sentences, the desire and its anticipated fulfillment joined. Had she wanted light, she would have said simply "I want light" in much the same tone as Jehovah's "Let there be light." In either case, there would be light. I don't mean she was spoiled or capricious, or that she expected to be waited on in her desires. "I want a girl" meant that she was about to embark on the process of adopting one; that she would overcome all obstacles with the firmness of her resolve and the resources at her disposal; and that her resolve and her resources were considerable.

"A servant?" Father misunderstood.

"No. Of course not. A girl of our own. A daughter."

"Oh."

"We'll have to adopt. You don't think I'm serious. I've thought about this."

"Okay." I have seen Father adopt this strategy before. The quick acquiescence to something of enormous moment, so that the burden of raising the obvious objections falls suddenly on the proposer.

Mother seemed not to have heard him. "Wouldn't it be nice to have a little girl?"

"Okay. Do it."

"Don't you want to think about it?"

"It's okay. Go ahead."

"We're talking about a person here. A change in our life."

"A daughter, to be specific. It's okay."

"You're bluffing. You don't think I'm serious. You think this is some post-menopausal burp or something. I'm serious. Don't pull that 'it's okay' shit with me."

"What shit? You want to adopt a girl. We need a coxswain for the family shell. Just make sure she's petite and not afraid of the water."

I didn't exactly witness this scene, of course. I'm imagining it, based on what I know of my parents' style of arguing. When we were growing up we used to Indian wrestle with Father. When we were very young, he would beat us by failing to counter our exertions, so that our own exuberance would throw us off balance. By the time we learned this stratagem we had moved on to other forms of competition.

Mother insisted we all come to dinner, and there she broke the news.

"You're going to have a sister." Unlike her desires, which were delivered in the imperative, her declarations always had a faint undertone of the interrogative.

I said, "You're pregnant? I thought . . ."

Mother saved me. "I am. Past menopause. We're adopting. Try to behave while we're in the process. You're the evidence that we're capable parents."

"Better go black market in that case." I don't remember who said this; it doesn't matter. We bantered about the unsuitableness of one or another of us as "evidence."

"Can't any of you be serious? I'm talking about your sister." Mother rose from the table at this point, as if she were going to propose a toast.

"To sister." I raised my glass.

"To sister." My brothers joined me. I think Father wanted to, but he knew better. Mother glared at each of us in turn. A look of such contempt, of such disgust, that it froze us in our spots. She left the table and did not return with dessert.

I'd seen this look before. It was Thanksgiving. The big dining room table groaning with food so perfect it looks lacquered. Pride of place goes to two huge turkeys, glazed to brown perfection. On their legs are these incredible lace doilies. I have no idea what they are called; you see them on rack of lamb. But these are more elaborate, they look like something you'd find in a poultry Victoria's Secret. This must be what Jake is thinking too, because when Mother hands him the carving knife and fork, and asks him to do the honors, he pauses. He stares at the turkey nearest him, draws our attention to it. He shakes his head. He puts the carving knife down. "I can't do it." Then he brightens. He grabs a leg in each hand and pulls them ever so gently apart. "But I'd love to take it upstairs and fuck the stuffing out of it."

Mother gives Jake a look of such withering contempt that it spawned its own name. After that Thanksgiving, whenever Mother got that look, we would caution each other: "Watch out for Mother: she's got that fuck-the-turkey look in her eyes."

★   ★   ★

On those occasions where he must dress up, Uncle Jake wears only women's clothes. No make-up, no wig. He doesn't shave his legs. I asked him why. "I like them. Besides it puts everyone else at their ease; makes them less defensive. See, Ty, everyone's worst social fear is humiliation. They realize that any humiliation that befalls them will pale in comparison, and they are put at ease." It was true; I never went to a bad party with Jake.

I liked to hang around Jake at parties because he attracted women. The debs, burnished bronze by the sun, mouths full of perfect white teeth, faces flush with daiquiris and yearning. Or so I imagined. The bravest would leave her clutch and approach Jake, as if on a dare.

"Hi, I'm Sandy." A hand offered at the end of a straight arm.

Jake takes the hand, which is expecting to be shaken, and brings it to his lips. "I'm Jake. Pleased to meet you, Sandy." Then the inevitable compliment. (And why not? Sandy is beautiful, or at least pretty; charming and willing to be charmed, dressed so as to elicit an honest compliment.) "You look stunning. The earrings, the earrings are perfect."

This creates a certain confusion in Sandy, who must, she feels, return the compliment. The self-possessed ones bring it off without a hitch: "You look perfect yourself."

If she says this with a wry smile, and doesn't convulse into girlish laughter, I find myself smitten.

The other debs walk over and Sandy introduces them.

They are dying to ask. What? They don't know exactly. They want an explanation. If you are disfigured, or lacking a limb, people want to know why. You owe us an explanation.

"This is Tyler."

Most of us here are Tylers. But it's my given name as well.

"Ty." I correct him. "Just Ty. Ty Tyler."

Again the straight arm, dangling a hand, from Sandy. I shake it. I am not my uncle.

"You're wondering, where do I shop?" Jake always meets their expectations obliquely. "The S_____ shop." (I can never remember the name, and besides, it changes.) "The first visit is always the most difficult. They have to be brought up to speed. 'What size? Who's it for?' the clerk asks. 'Size twelve. For me.' There's usually a stand-off at this point, although the better New York shops take it in stride. But in this case it's a first, because the clerk repeats herself. Brightens actually. 'Who's going to wear it?' I'm such a kidder, she thinks.

"'I am. I'm going to wear it.' Now she's flustered. She's looking for a catch, a way out. She sees one.

'Are you from one of those TV shows?' She's looking over my shoulder for an accomplice. 'What is this?'

" 'This is a man, attempting to buy a gown, to wear to his nephew's wedding. This doesn't happen very often, but it's happening now. It takes a little getting used to. The better shops offer their customers a little sherry. Perhaps you could join me in a glass.' "

"Would you like a drink? Can I get you a drink?"

Sandy wants a drink, or wants rather, to accept his offer of hospitality, but doesn't want to stop the story.

I say: "I'll get drinks. Daiquiris okay?"

Jake continues: "I say to the clerk ' I do this all the time, but you don't. I'm discerning, but I won't waste your time. I'd like to spend about two grand, but if we see something extraordinary, more is okay. Okay?' Sometimes the mention of money helps ground them."

Sandy's look says her gown cost considerably less than two grand. Jealousy or awe? I like Sandy. Let it be awe.

I said I'd get drinks but I don't. I stay to watch the rest of Sandy's reactions.

Look in vain for some defining instant that set Jake on his course of wearing dresses. Some childhood humiliation. Some adolescent misadventure. If you must have a reason, imagine this: Jake is thirteen, and is dressed as a girl for a costume party. The young lady of his current desire is disarmed by his sheep's clothing; a brief and poignant sexual encounter ensues – well, you get the picture: dresses are lucky for Jake. It never happened.

*   *   *

We are at the funeral home, making the arrangements. The pressing issue is this: what is the corpse to wear? A dark funerary suit, of course. I was sent to Uncle's pied-a-terre to retrieve the mortuary togs. I wanted to loiter among his private papers. I didn't. I went straight to his closet, mindful of my purpose. Forget black: there wasn't a suit of any color. Nothing but dresses, not even a pantsuit such as a smart young female broker might wear to a weekend lunch with a client. I reported back the news.

"Well, we'll close the coffin." Mother, ever the practical one, to the funeral director.

"As you wish. But he still has to wear something."

I was dying to ask why. I imagine the thought of being naked at his own funeral would have pleased Jake. Of course he would have wanted an open casket in that case.

"We'll have a suit made." It fell to Mother to enforce the proprieties. She swam the English Channel as a younger woman; getting a suit made in a day for a dead man didn't seem like much of an obstacle. She was reduced, after a dozen calls, to complaining that nowadays there were a few things money couldn't buy.

"Just put him in the Halston and close the damn casket." My Father.

The Halston cost four or five grand, and I knew Mother intended to auction it for charity. She had always thought it needlessly extravagant and the auction was the chance to redeem it in her eyes. She wasn't about to stick it in the ground.

"Not the Halston."

"What then? Just panty hose and a bra?"

"The Halston's a red herring. Face the issue: is he going to be buried as a man or a woman?"

"He's a man. We can't do anything about that. The issue is his clothing."

"Had he left instructions, he would have insisted on a dress. Probably the Halston."

"We would have a judge vacate that request."

"Probably not." My brother, one of several family lawyers, corrected Mother.

The funeral parlor has recessed lighting, like an airplane's. How appropriate. The funeral director is an unctuous man smelling of too much after shave. Polo, in our honor. Jake would have called him on it.

"May I make a suggestion?" The funeral director is addressing Mother.

"No." Then to me: "Get one of your suits."

"Won't fit." And not fitting.

Mother glares at each of us in turn: me, my brother James (the lawyer of the unfavorable legal opinion),

Father, Polo the Funeral Director. Finally at Jake. The "fuck-the-turkey" look.

★ ★ ★

Mother swam the Channel from Calais to Dover, recapitulating a journey her ancestors had made shortly after 1066. They used boats. Six hundred years later a branch of her family crossed the Atlantic, starved, froze, endured and planted their family on New World soil. The family flourished: it sprouted farmers and ministers; then judges, statesmen, physicians, bankers and the occasional black sheep. It was a predominantly male line: some anomaly in the sperm or the conjugal habits yielded mostly men. I have three brothers. Father, as I've said, has three brothers. Father likes the idea of adopting a girl because the eight of us – he and his brothers, me and mine – could crew a family shell, but we lack a coxswain. A petite girl would be perfect.

"We are adopting a child, not a part of a boat." Mother.

But I see what my father sees: eight sturdy Tylers, two generations at the oars, average weight 205 pounds, ruddy with exertion, pulling together to the cadence called by a porcelain complexioned girl, her ponytail gathered in a silver clasp. He sees it like a picture, gilt framed, above the mantel, emblematic of everything he hopes we are.

You would think it a simple thing for a wealthy, connected family to adopt a child. Mother chooses an agency specializing in Asian children, because she's been advised the process is less complicated. But my parents learn at the adoption agency that they are old.

"How old are you?"

Mother sees the trap: "Old enough to raise a child." She is not used to being a supplicant; she doesn't know the forms.

The agency woman, young, heavy, frowns. "The ideal candidate is between thirty and forty. Studies show . . ."

Mother waves her off, but the agency woman continues her theme.

"Have you the energy to keep up with an active child? Most people think these children are docile, especially the girls, they've seen too many bad movies with that polite oriental stereotype. But children are children. Little children are particularly active."

"Oh. I'm so glad you told me. I thought we'd just put her in the display case. It worked so well with my boys." Mother's anger is formidable. The mercy she generally shows the world ceases to flow; in its place a laser guided vitriol searches for its mark. "How many children have you raised?"

"I have two kids."

"That's not what I asked. How many have you raised? How many have reached adulthood."

"What?" The agency woman does not understand.

Mother presses: "How many? How many adults?"

"My children are four and six."

"Mine are 22, 24, 27 and 30. Adult, alive, healthy, courteous, responsible. When you can say the same, in twenty years, if at all, you can pass judgment on my fitness as a parent."

Father is watching this with growing mortification. She's tipped the boat here. No coxswain will come of this exchange.

Later, in the privacy of the elevator, he says: "You certainly showed her."

"Do you think she hates us because we're white?"

"No, she hates us because we're rich."

Father had repaired a few breaches in his day, and was assessing the damage. Mother's harangue, while sharp, was essentially defensive. She had made no accusations or disparagements. That was good. It would play well when repeated and the tone declawed. He was already imagining the conversation with the adoption worker's supervisor. Mother's anger would become upset – not a calculated attack, but an over-flowing from an internal wound. He was envisioning a hierarchy he would ascend, and with each step in that ascension his wife would become more the aggrieved party, until at the apex he would be face to face with someone as reasonable as he was. If not, at least then he would be free to lock horns with his adversary without feeling like a bully.

★ ★ ★

Not fit? Not fit? You could look on a globe, any globe, a small cheap one and see the English Channel, a visible blue distance, and she had crossed it. Not fit? You could stand on the moon and see that separation from a quarter of a million miles away. Not fit indeed.

We are not a family of athletes. Rather we are perseverance incarnate, and sometimes that takes the form of athletics. So we tend to run and to row and to swim, activities too boring for real athletes. Our perseverance may be the virtue we make of a certain dullness, the reassurance we find in repetition. Mother with her oars of flesh, sculling across the Channel; father, uncles, brothers, plying our wooden oars. Sisyphean sports. Unwatchable sports.

Hardly Aphrodite. Mother standing in the foam at Dover. Her arms and thighs thick. A smile, but her eyes vague with fatigue. Her lips swollen and cracked. Splotches of Crisco, all that remains of her coating. As ugly a picture as she has ever taken. The record of the event.

$$\star \quad \star \quad \star$$

I won't take you through all the stations of the cross, which is how Father began to refer to the adoption process. We'll just fast forward to the meeting with the agency head. The crisis that morning was what to wear. Normally, this is not a problem; we are well versed in what is appropriate for all occasions. If you were visiting a self-important bureaucrat on official business you wore a conservative blue suit and a rep tie, something that would flatter his sense of solemn importance. Nothing too fancy, nothing Italian, nothing that would work against the phony seriousness of the occasion. But because we are wealthy, Father was afraid such a suit might take on an intimidating connotation. The sun was beginning to grill up a hot, unpleasant day. Father decided to wear the blue suit, but to carry the jacket and loosen the tie: proof that he could feel the heat just like the next man, suffer it in a democracy of men made equal by common sweat.

Mother eschewed her jewelry for this occasion; not even a watch, since time as well as money was the enemy. The thought of dyeing her hair had crossed her mind; she quickly obliterated the thought. She wore the most sensible looking shoes she could find.

The meeting was in one of those ponderous federal buildings. Its architecture matched its purpose: Monolithic blocky concrete with some whimsical touches that were intended to signal a humanity it didn't possess and could only guess at. It had guessed wrong.

The elevator hoisted them to their appointment. The Director of Adoption Services was a thin black woman with a military carriage. She wore a single strand of pearls, identical to the ones Mother had left at home. (According to Father, Mother had all she could do not to call home and make sure hers were still in the jewelry case.)

Mrs. Starks did not offer to shake hands. She indicated they should sit in the two chairs facing her desk. There was nothing on her desk, not even a phone. An index card with the word "IN" on it was taped to the corner. Father was recalibrating his opening remarks. He decided to let Ms. Starks go first.

"Mr. and Mrs. Tyler. Repeat after me: 'I am fifty-six; Li is two. When Li is twelve, I will be sixty-six. When Li is eighteen, I will be seventy-two.' You see the problem?"

Father says: "I see the prejudice."

The thing is, people don't wither under clever retorts, like they do in the movies. They just keep going. Father knows this; his remark escaped the usual vigilance he held over his speech.

"'When Li is eighteen, I will be seventy-two.' Just say it. I'm serious. Just say it."

Mother said: "When Li is eighteen, I will be seventy-two. When Li is one hundred and eighteen, I'll be one hundred and seventy-two. I'm sorry. I understand your point. I just don't agree with it."

"I'm sorry. I'm sorry you don't agree with it. Don't you want what's best for this child, even if what's best isn't you?"

The meeting seesawed back and forth, and grew less heated. Each side made small conciliatory gestures to the other's fundamental decency. They parted on decent terms, but without a child.

It was Jake who found May. "I got you a little girl. She needs a little work. She's four years old. May. May is her name." Mother was visiting him in the hospital, where he lay ravished by chemotherapy. Thin, without hair, he looked like a skull over which a nylon stocking had been stretched. Mother did not understand at first. "Her name is May. Your daughter."

How had he managed this, when all her resources, all her perseverance, had failed. She said simply, "How?"

"I cheated, of course. Still, the adoption, when you and John sign the papers, will be legal."

"How?"

"A million dollars and a future draft pick."

Later Mother would say he made some sort of deal with the devil. His arbitrageur of choice.

★ ★ ★

Mother summoned me and my brothers to a dinner, to meet May. Mother had prepared an elaborate Chinese meal, which I learned was actually Vietnamese. We ate in the formal dining room, which dwarfed the spring rolls and lemon chicken as it had never dwarfed the hams and turkeys.

"May escaped Vietnam on a boat not much bigger than this table. And less sturdy." Mother intended by this remark to enlist our sympathy for our new sister. It wasn't necessary: we were long past the age of tormenting the newest family members. May's problem would come from the opposite direction: we were all old enough to be her father and she would be smothered in an avalanche of affection.

★   ★   ★

Jake died while I was away at college: my junior year abroad, in England. I meant to come home sooner. But we believe this of those we are fond of: they will last forever, or at least as long as we need them. I was old enough to know better and should have come sooner.

I flew first class. Jake would have approved. "You're rich; that's the simple fact. You didn't earn it, so you don't have to apologize for it. You're just a winner in life's lottery. It's a state of grace; live gracefully. Do good if you see the opportunity, but include yourself. I can't stand these rich folks who ride around in Fords and fly tourist to prove that money hasn't spoiled them. Money spoils you. Bear it like a man."

The stewardess was solicitous. People often ask the time of me, or directions. I have an approachable demeanor. It was Jake who pointed this out to me. We were in New York, walking down Fifth Avenue. A striking young lady stopped us. "Do you have the time?" Later I thought of a dozen clever responses; but I was surprised and answered honestly: "Yes." I looked at my wrist. "It's three-twenty." She paused, thanked me, and was gone. Jake saw me puff up a bit

– like I said, the woman was striking – and she had picked me to ask the time of. I was seventeen. Jake said, "Easy Tiger. All she wanted was the time. And you look like the sort of decent guy who would give it to her without making her fish in your pants for a pocket watch." Seeing my wounded look, he added, "Sometimes the decent guys get the beautiful girls; it just takes them a little longer. This isn't the movies." The next day I received a package. A pocket watch and a note: "A more generous uncle, in a different century, would have sent you the girl."

The stewardess had that British knack of serving without being the least bit servile. "Going home for the Holidays, Yank?" My drinking had made her familiar. It was curious.

"No. A funeral."

"So sorry."

"Yeah. Me too."

"Someone close?"

"My favorite uncle. Taught me all the manly arts. Cards, pool, playing the horses, drinking, smoking."

She patted my arm. The wine, and the drone of the flight, made me sleepy. I dozed.

This is how Jake died: Slowly, with frequent bouts of hope, from pancreatic cancer. There was nothing particularly meaningful about Jake dying from this, rather than living, or dying in some other fashion. The nurses adored him; it was like the debs all over again. He was witty to the very end, for them. To

Mother, he said, in a lucid moment of despair, "Do you believe this shit?" He was referring to the accoutrements of the final stage of his illness – the Levine tube, the catheter, the IV.

★   ★   ★

In the end, it was the Halston. You knew it would be. It fit poorly on his wasted body. We closed the casket. For Jake's sake, and for ours. He would not have wanted to be seen that way. He looked pathetic in it. But not everything that looks ridiculous is wrong.

Father commissioned a portrait of the Tylers crewing their eight. It is, when you get down to it, a portrait of Jake. He isn't in it; his spot is empty; his oar is shipped. The painter has softened May somewhat; you have to look very hard to see the disfigurement. Her face is shaded by a baseball cap, her black hair spraying out the back. Mother has given it pride of place: it hangs over the mantel in the library.

Tag Sale

"Bright and early, boychick." The implication is that he will get up before me for the joint tag sale we've planned for tomorrow. "He" is Hyman. A guy in his late fifties, maybe early sixties. Not quite old enough to be my father, though he likes to act the part. My neighbor, Hyman Skolnick. A piece of work.

I'm not looking forward to it. The tag sale. It's hot now – still – though it's evening. It was hot all day. It's supposed to be even hotter tomorrow. And humid. We're looking forward to a jungle of a day with stale, sticky air. Miami at its worst. Our quiet cul-de-sac will be filled with lowlifes. I will have to put up with their haggling, and the sob stories they'll tell in support of their haggling, and with Hy. And the sticky heat too. Hy will relish it all, of course.

Our cul-de-sac is four large homes, done in the hacienda style, with orange tile roofs and stucco walls. Fake balconies, suggested by wrought iron grillwork, reach halfway up each window. There are tall palm trees at regular intervals in front of the homes. These always look unnatural to me, with their rigid symmetry. Hyman's house is next to ours.

Hy has backed his Lincoln out of the garage to wash it. He's wearing a sleeveless T-shirt and cut off jeans. And slippers. The part of his back I can see is covered with curly, black hair. He's a big guy, a bear. He has curly, black hair on his knuckles. Like I said, a piece of work.

"Pull your car over, boychick. We'll wash it."

"No thanks." I wave Hy off. I categorically refuse all of Hy's offers. He's always making me offers I can refuse:

"Boychick, let's go to Hialeah."

"Boychick, let's take our cars out on I-95 and open 'em up."

"Boychick, let's go down to South Beach and look at the *feygellahs*." You get the picture. Oh, and my favorite:

"Boychick, let's go to Wolfie's for some lime Jell-o." Translucent green cubes in a thick sundae glass. Hy's favorite dessert.

Now, here's the thing. Hy is rich. He made his money in the diaper business. "Boychick, I turn shit into gold." He says it without irony, all the time, like he has just minted the expression. Hearing him say it you don't think of the metaphor, but of him sitting in some dark room, like Rumplestiltskin, literally making the transformation.

Here's another thing: Hy's wife. Allison is young and gorgeous. Okay, he's rich, it happens. But she's a professor at the U of M. He looks like a Neanderthal. She's chairperson of the anthropology department. Figure that out.

Anyway, here's how they met. He took her class. Never been to college; but he gets it in his head to take a class at the university. "Hey boychick, want to take a class with me?" I was so surprised, I almost forgot to decline. I didn't even ask what class. Next time I see him, he says, "Boychick, you should have taken that class. That professor, she's a looker." He sticks out in class like some bear wandering among the flamingos. She notices him. Actually she notices him because of an ugly scene. He asks a question. Some kid sniggers. Actually several kids snigger, but one kid sniggers louder than the rest.

"What's so funny?"

"You man, you're unbelievable."

"What's your name?"

"Marty."

"Marty what?"

"Marty Helfstein."

Hy says, "Marty Helfstein, Coral Gables, right?" The kid nods, wonders, where is this going? "I was your diaper man." Everybody gets set for them to drop the hostility. See there's a connection.

Marty says, "What?" What is this geezer talking about?

Hy says, "I was your diaper man, your mom used my diaper service. She was so worried about you. She would always ask me, 'It's so little, are all the boys' things that little?'" There is an uneasy incomprehension on Marty's face. "So Marty, how did that little dick of yours turn out?"

Well maybe it goes on a little longer between them. Who knows? Hy always stops the story with him having the last word. Anyway, the professor catches him at the end of class, wants to talk to him. "Boychick, the rest is history." Like his charm is so obvious that he has only to get face-to-face with this beautiful, intelligent woman for her to fall in love with him. But that's what happened. "Our first date, we went to see Othello. That's what did it." He had to divorce his first wife; that was loud and ugly.

I go into my house, to escape Hy and the heat. I ask Janice if she wants to help out with the sale. I say, "It'll be fun" to the sound of Janice knocking around in the kitchen. Janice doesn't say anything, she just comes into the foyer and pantomimes a guy jerking off, a couple of pumps aimed at her crotch. I taught her that gesture. Janice can be pretty funny if you're not the one it's aimed at.

She says: "I put the stuff I want to get rid of in shopping bags. On the table for now. Is The

Baby-Sitter going to help?" The Baby-Sitter is Janice's name for Allison.

"How many bags?"

"Five. I'm having lunch with your mother, so I don't have to have her for dinner. You've got the better deal, even with Hy thrown in."

Janice doesn't like my mother, for the usual daughter-in-law reasons, but she hates Hy because he dumped his first wife. Hy's first wife, she was a piece of work too, a female version of Hy. A talker. A screamer, really.

I go into the kitchen to see what Janice has put in the bags. She asks again: "Is The Baby-sitter going to help?" Allison is The Baby-Sitter because she looks about sixteen and wears her long blonde hair in a ponytail.

"Who cares?" This is stupid on my part. We both care.

"I wish you didn't care. But you do. So I do."

"I don't think she's going to help. Why should she? I wish I wasn't working the sale."

"She's not your type, you know."

"Who is my type?"

"Not her. I am. I'm your type. But sometimes you're such a putz you forget it." Janice leaves the foyer, and then comes back. "If she works the sale I'm going to have to blow off your mother to keep an eye on you."

"Tell me, while you're at it, what does she see in him?"

"What do any of us see in any of you? I'll tell you what she sees in Hy: his flat-out adoration of her. You should try it some time. None of this 'I love you only as much as you love me' shit. He's a fool for her."

"Are you attracted to Hy?" I know the answer, but I like to hear Janice go off on Hy.

"Are you kidding? But I can see why Allison is. He brought flowers to her in class, like she was a prima ballerina."

"You're kidding."

"You didn't know that. She told me. She was embarrassed, or she pretended to be when she told me. She loved it. So this is how Hy operates: he doesn't worry about 'Does she like him?' He wants something, he goes after it. He says to himself, 'What do I have to do, how much, how long, to make this woman love me?' Doesn't doubt for a minute that eventually she'll fall for him. Can you see how confident this is? Can you see how Allison might fall for him? Can you see how that might be attractive to a woman who chooses to live among primitive cultures, so her discomfort with her own culture won't show? You think it's great she's an anthropologist; I'm telling you it's a cover for her own insecurity. Good night."

I go up to bed late; Janice is already asleep.

★   ★   ★

I get up early, early for a Saturday; but when I look out, Hy is already setting up. I shower quickly and skip breakfast.

"Boychick, have a donut."

I watch what I eat. I haven't eaten a jelly donut since I was a kid.

"You want some coffee? Go in and have Allison pour you a cup. Have a donut."

I would like to have Allison pour me a cup of coffee. We'll see about the donut.

I'm glad that I showered, but my skin is already damp from the brief conversation with Hy. We are out of our fucking minds to be having a tag sale today. We should just call the Salvation Army and have them haul this shit away.

I go up to Hy's door and knock. Hy yells, "Go on in, it's open." I'm not comfortable just walking in on his wife. That's why I knocked in the first place.

Allison opens the door before I have to explain this to Hy. She's got a towel wrapped around her head and she smells pleasantly of soap.

"Give boychick some coffee," Hy yells at Allison.

When we're inside I ask her, "Are you going to help with the tag sale? It'll be like fieldwork for you." I always make a point of acknowledging Allison's professorial credentials. Allison seems not to have understood the reference. Then she says: "How do you take your coffee?'

"Black. Thank you."

Allison pours me some coffee and then offers me some cream and sugar. "Black," I remind her.

Then she says, "No. I'm not going to work the tag sale." I am always looking at Allison for some clue that she understands the irony of her marriage to Hyman. She either doesn't get it or refuses to share it with me.

I would like to stay in the cool house with Allison, but I've run out of conversation. I don't have much to say in the morning. I take the coffee outside. The heat hits me like a curtain. Hy hands me a jelly donut. I start eating; I don't even think about it.

Hy has already schlepped a few things out to the front. His forehead glistens. His black curly hair, what's left of it, lies pasted to his scalp. It looks faintly Roman. Jelly from my donut squeezes out onto the driveway. I start looking for a place to throw it away. A wave of irritation passes through me. A fucking jelly donut.

I put my coffee cup down on Hy's table and start to carry my own stuff out to the front. It's 8:30; it's already 95 degrees out. Two trips and I'm soaking wet.

"Hy," I say, "Why are we doing this?"

"Boychick, we'll make it fun. Here's what we'll do. We'll make a bet; who sells the most."

I don't want to make it fun. I don't say anything to encourage Hy.

I don't need to. He's warming to his own idea. "Here's the bet. Winner keeps all the money from the sale. Yours and mine. Loser has to run around the cul-de-sac with no clothes on."

The thought of Hy running around the cul-de-sac naked almost makes me lose my jelly donut. I say "Hy, if you'll stay out here and sell my stuff you can keep the money." Hy frowns. He's always disappointed in my lack of playfulness.

He says: "Forget about running around with no clothes. I forgot how shy you are." He means modest. I'm not shy. Besides he got the idea from me. We were trading war stories. I sometimes do that, spend a few minutes trading stories with Hy, when I decline one of his offers. I told him this story:

"The software company I work for flies us down to Half Moon Bay, Jamaica, for a week-long sales meeting. We scuba, we golf, we pretend to do a little work. We drink. Anyway, on one particular day, we're playing volleyball on the beach. It's all sales reps, so it's real competitive. Volleyball, and we're going to play for world domination. Losing team has to go into the water and take their bathing suits off; hold them over their heads. We play hard. We argue childishly over out-of-bounds calls. We lose. We run into the water until it's over our waists. We face the beach, take off our trunks, hold them over our heads, semaphores of defeat. Now one of the reps on our team is a woman. And she's game. She splashes into the water with the rest of us. She takes off her bikini bottom and holds it over her head. Shouts of approval. Then 'Margo, take off your top.' This is a gray area."

I paused in my story. I saw Hy liked this story, even though he wasn't telling it. "So she takes off her top?" Hy asked. I can tell he wanted her to. I smiled. I waited a beat, then I go on.

"People on both teams are screaming at her: 'Margo, if you don't take off your top you'll never play volleyball in this town again.' Hy is getting ready to interrupt again, but I cut him off: "Here's what she does: she turns her back to the beach and then she takes off her top. Holds it over head. Wild cheers from the beach and water."

I made up the last part. Margo doesn't take off her top, not really. It just makes the story better if she does.

Hy nods approvingly. Then he tells me about the diaper business:

"The local paper prints birth announcements, right, boychick? I wait a few days and then I call: 'Can I bring a gift by? No obligation.' I stop by the next day. I got gifts. Something for the baby, something for the mother. I never wear a suit. Who comes to your door in a suit? The FBI, Jehovah's Witnesses, politicians, that's who. I go in, I refuse coffee if it's offered – otherwise I'd be pissing every stop – I present the gifts. I ask to see the baby. Then I shock 'em: I drape my shoulder with a Pamper, glossy side out, and I make like I'm gonna place their baby against that nasty plastic surface. This is the key, boychick: make them hurt, then make them better, the fundamental rule of salesmanship. The mother, she's about to *plotz*. She grows eyes as big as saucers and runs looking for a burp cloth. I catch myself, make a joke of my goof – imagine burping a baby against a Pamper – and I materialize a cloth diaper like a magician. Everybody's happy now, the baby, the mother. The baby goes instantly mellow. I tell 'em: 'Don't throw out your disposables. You'll always need a few for trips and situations where real diapers aren't practical. Now, everybody's scared of diaper pins, right? We don't use pins.' Out comes my patented diaper tape with pictures of pink-and-blue-headed safety pins printed on it. 'As easy as a disposable. Better for the baby. Better for the ecology.' Then I change the baby.

"Occasionally, I get a gusher. A male who sends up a fountain from his little changing table. Guaranteed maximum sale. Seventy-two diapers a week."

Who in their right mind would make a bet with a guy like this? But here's Hy, his hairy paw extended to me: "So boychick, we got a bet?" I slap my hands to get rid of some of the powdered sugar. We shake. We have a bet.

I admit it gives me some pleasure to see the light in Hy's eyes. I'm always declining his offers, and I know this disappoints him. I always envy Hy, that his feelings come to him so undiluted. His hand is moist. When I get my hand back there's a caulking of powdered sugar in the creases.

I don't like to lose. So I try to become indifferent to the heat. Hy is a good sport. Even though we are competitors now, he instructs Allison to bring us both iced tea at regular intervals. I would prefer beer, but Hy doesn't drink. Go figure.

The day, as I said is sultry. The first car pulls up at 8:45. "No early birds," I call. But Hy grins and says "Step right up."

Hy's wearing a short apron, like concessionaires wear at the ball games, with JEWISH WAR VETERANS in white on its blue background. He has on his half glasses, which make him look grandfatherly. Allison brings him an iced tea, and asks me if I want one. I do.

By noon the good stuff is all gone. We observe the folkways of poker: we don't count our money since the game isn't over.

A couple in a light utility truck drives up. He's tall and ponytailed. She's thin, her face all angles under black hair. They want a coffeemaker. Hy disappears into his house and returns with a fairly new one.

He offers up the coffeemaker. The remnants of the morning coffee are still in it. "Twenty bucks. It cost me seventy new."

The woman whispers to her partner. Then, "I'll give you ten."

Then Hy does his number. "Eighteen. If you buy it, and you think you made a bad deal, you can always resell it for twenty, which is what we both know it's worth. But if I take it back into the house, you'll have to buy one new and pay fifty for one that's not half as good. Or you can drive around until you find one that probably doesn't work for ten bucks. You know this one is good because you can still smell the coffee."

The couple confers. "Twelve."

Hy starts to take it back into the house.

"Fifteen," the angular woman calls after him.

Hy stops, but doesn't turn. "Fifteen." She shouts it this time.

Hy shrugs his back at them, but then he turns and brings them the coffeemaker.

When the transaction is concluded, and they've left, I say to Hy "I thought the bet was just for the stuff for the tag sale." I should have known better. Hy shoots me a look back that's full of mischief. Of course, with Hy, there are no rules. In the heat of the competition he might run into my house, sell my things, the son of a bitch.

I start with the marginal stuff. Stuff we still use, but hope to replace. A five year old toaster oven, still in good shape: ten dollars.

"You got any dishes?" A kid needing a shave in an orange University of Miami T-shirt.

"I got dishes, boychick."

"I've got dishes." I couldn't believe I'm saying this. I run into the house for my dishes. They aren't new. Ten years old. But they have served us well enough. It takes me two trips to carry them out: dinner plates, dessert plates, bowls. I tell the kid thirty dollars.

He stares, uncomprehendingly. Of course he's never bought dishes in his life. He has no idea if I'm screwing him or not.

"They cost two hundred dollars new."

"Twenty-five?" It's a question.

I nod; take the money. Hy gives me a thumbs up sign. Then he goes inside and comes back with a handmade sign: "If You Don't See What You Want, Ask!!!"

I make my own sign: "Estate Sale. Everything Must Go!"

I begin to suspect that Hy has put something in the iced tea. Or maybe in the jelly donut. The heat, it has to be over one hundred degrees. I feel like I'm in a spacesuit, something that muffles everything and creates its own climate. I no longer feel uncomfortable, just strange, buried deep within myself. I remove my sunglasses, put them on top of my head. The day is gleaming; everything seems to be made of chrome. Our cul-de-sac is on fire with this chrome light. I sell the stuff that's easy to carry out first. Small appliances: electric can opener, coffee maker, Mixmaster, popcorn popper, waffle iron, electric toothbrush, cordless phone, clock-radio, coffee grinder. I'm barely aware of Hy. The cul-de-sac was starting to fill up with people and cars. I suddenly have an overwhelming need to know the time. I look at my watch – my first thought is to sell it – it's after 3.

Lew saunters over. Lew lives on the other side of Hy.

"Look, boychick, it's the Medicine Man." Lew owns a local chain of drugstores. He's a tall trim man, a shape well suited to cut through the thick south Florida air. He has on tennis whites, a visor, shades.

"You guys moving?"

I detect irony in the question, but Hy takes it literally. "No no no, just having a little tag sale." Hy winks at me; our bet is our secret, our bond.

"Lew, did you bring your wallet?"

There's a slight hesitation to Lew's smile. He's trying to figure it out.

Hy says, "Join the fun Lew. Sweat a little. Buy something."

Lew looks as if he might. Buy something, not sweat. Lew looks immune to the heat that has Hy and me sweating like pigs.

"How much for the kayak?" Hy has a kayak.

"I only used it once. I bought it for Allison. She never got the hang of it."

Three lies in a row. Hy bought it for himself. He practically lived in it for a week, and then he abandoned it for his next enthusiasm. Allison could make it fly through the water.

"How much?"

"Lew, for you, one hundred bucks."

"How much for somebody else?" Lew isn't taking any chances.

"It cost five hundred dollars new." This may have been true, but I doubt it.

Lew objects. "It's plastic."

"Space-age plastic. No-maintenance plastic. Won't-rot-or-mildew plastic. Light-weight plastic."

Lew takes out his wallet. He looks inside and frowns. "I've got twenty-three dollars." Then he brightens, like he just had a great idea. "Will you take twenty-three dollars?"

Hy can't believe it. "Lew, you live next door. Go inside and get seventy-seven dollars more."

Lew asks "Do you take credit cards?"

"It's a fucking tag sale, Lew, not Neiman Marcus."

"It's plastic," Lew says again, hoping maybe this time it isn't. "I wish it were wood. A nice wooden kayak."

Hy asks, "You want some iced tea, Lew?"

"I'd really like a wooden kayak. Is the paddle wood?"

The paddle is plastic too.

"Lew, when I come to your store and get my prescription filled, do I get a nice wooden pill box? Because I would really like a nice wooden pill box.

No. I get little plastic bottles with little plastic tops I can't open. It's plastic, Lew. Go into your house and get the rest of the money."

"It's hot out here." Lew says this to me. Like he just figured that out. "If I go back inside I don't think I'll come back out. Too damn hot. How can you guys stand it?" Then to Hy. "Is that kayak still plastic? Have you got a wooden model?"

Lew goes back into his house. It finally dawns on Hy that Lew wasn't going to buy his kayak, that he's just been yanking his chain. "Boychick, do you believe that *momzer*?"

I tell Hy that it looks like our tea service is leaving. Allison is locking the door. Then she gets into her Miata – his birthday present to her, Hy has let me know – and pulls out of the driveway without waving. Her license plate says "Save the Manatees."

"Boychick, she's pissed."

Hy seems puzzled. I know Allison's reaction is mild compared to what my own wife's will be. I think about offering Hy fifty bucks for the kayak. Then I can sell it to Lew for a hundred, who will buy it from me just to get a rise out of Hy.

"Hy, I'll give you fifty bucks for the kayak. More if you can turn it into wood."

Hy looks like a bear that has been cornered by dogs. About to explode, but choosing a direction to explode into. But he keeps his cool. "Seventy-five."

I tell him, "Not a penny over fifty." I know how badly Hy wants to sell that kayak – needs to sell it – now that he's been jerked around by Lew.

Hy frowns. "Okay, boychick. But throw in your wife's exercise trampoline."

We have a deal. I don't have the heart to go resell the kayak to Lew. Not right at that moment.

I ask Hy,"When is this over?"

"What?"

"The tag sale."

"How about midnight?" He's serious. "We could go later." Then he brightens. "Or when everything is sold."

Hy doesn't wait for my reply. He goes to the front door, finds it locked, goes around to the back. He comes back with silverware, which he begins polishing with an old diaper.

I go in and get our silverware. Stainless, really. More modern looking, I mean more contemporary, than Hy's. Hy's is heavy, thick-handled stuff, with an ornate design. New Orleans whorehouse silverware.

I have never in my life thought about my silverware. But I feel a sad tug, a kind of constriction in my chest, when I bring ours out. It's ten years old. It was a wedding gift. I ate with it last night. I have a dim notion I should pass it on to my kids, though of course they won't want it.

Miss Lew sticks her head out of Lew's door. Miss Lew is Lew's mother. Dyed hair, pedal pushers, rhinestones on every available article of clothing. She was tight with Hy's first wife, a kind of surrogate mother-daughter thing. Anyway, they used to cry together when Hy took up with Allison. She coached Hy's wife through the divorce. Miss Lew would come out every morning when Hy left for work and smack his Lincoln with a broom. Whacked his car like she meant it too. The first time, Hy made the mistake of powering down the window. "Feh," Miss Lew said and spit air at him. After that he ran the gauntlet with his windows up. "Boychick," Hy said to me at the time, "That's the only time that yenta has ever used a broom in her life. I'm surprised she knows which end to hold."

This is true. Usually it's Bonita, their Ecuadorian housekeeper, who does the broom handling. My wife says that watching Miss Lew whack Hy's Lincoln is the reason she gets up in the morning.

Anyway, it's Miss Lew, broomless, that's on her way over now. She has to go by Hy first. She stops, fehs, spits air, and walks on toward me.

"How much?" She's tapping the silverware with four fingers. Now the thing is, I don't want to sell my silverware to Miss Lew. I don't know why. I can't even believe she's out here. She's diehard Neiman Marcus. Wouldn't go near a tag sale. Something's amiss here. I don't know what to say. "How much did you say?" Miss Lew demands of me. I haven't said anything.

"One hundred dollars." Formal. I'm not sure the word "bucks" is in Miss Lew's vocabulary. "Bucks" is the currency the lower stations use. I don't know what to expect. Will she haggle?

Miss Lew pulls a small purse from her pocketbook. She tries a couple of different compartments. Then she pulls out a bill, folded about a hundred times like an accordion. A hundred dollar bill. She unfolds it and smoothes out the wrinkles and hands it to me. I know I should offer to carry the silverware to her house, but the offer dies in my throat. Miss Lew gets me off the hook. "I'll send Bonita over later to pick it up."

I catch Hy's eye and hold Miss Lew's hundred dollar bill up like a cue card. Hy eventually gets fifty dollars for his silverware from a Haitian woman who makes him count every piece of it.

We start clearing out our houses a room at a time. And we settle into, are forced into, a crude auction. There are lots of people now; a small mob fills our cul-de-sac, eager for a bargain. Somehow the word has travelled, this is no ordinary tag sale where all the good stuff is gone by 9:30. So I auction off a room full of furniture, while Hy and a deputized helper haul a room full of chairs and tables and lamps and rugs out. Then he auctions while I go in and empty out the next room in my house. We are into it now. The heat is irrelevant now. We are beyond it, in some sacred place. The eager faces before me. Hy doing his damnedest. The police with flashers going at the end of the street. The Cuban station playing salsa – we are out of our minds.

I'm holding a wad of money in my hand now; it won't fit in my pocket. It's as fat as an apple, with the suede-like finish of much-handled bills. I can see something bright in the eyes of the people I make change for.

Hy takes it to the next level. "'Price is Right!'" he yells. "'Price is Right' Closest to original price gets a ten dollar voucher!" He's establishing value, the sly bastard. The crowd loves it. Everybody shouts a price. Nobody can help themselves. He brings out his pièce de résistance, his big gun, his main attraction: the wide-screen TV. The fifty-inch model. Someone yells "nine hundred dollars!" and the crowd boos him. An ignoramus. Everyone knows a big screen TV like that, a fifty-inch model, that's at least $1,299. Who knows what Hy paid for it? He gives a ten dollar voucher to a plump and pretty Hispanic woman and starts the bidding at two hundred. It climbs quickly to three seventy-five, falters briefly, and then another flurry drives it to four-seventy. To the man in the visor. I think for a moment it's Lew, the Medicine Man. But it's not.

"Will you take a check?" the visor asks.

"Sure," says Hy. "Will you take a note promising you the TV when your check clears?"

The man with the visor thinks about that, then says, "Okay."

★ ★ ★

It's after six, still light, still hot, when Janice returns. She's frantic. She asks if I'm alright and hugs me, clings to me like something might try to take me away if she let go. "I saw the police and the cars and I thought–God, I don't know what I thought." I tell her I'm okay. I tell her the police were there to help with the traffic, that a lot of people showed up for the sale. She gives me a final squeeze, but isn't ready to let go entirely. She holds my hand and leads me into our house. I feel empty, like my insides had been suddenly sucked dry by some invisible creature. Her panic returns and she hugs me again. "We've been robbed. Why didn't you say so?"

I shake my head. "I sold it. In the tag sale."

"Who are you?" Janice screams. "Who the fuck are you?" She goes upstairs to our bedroom. I follow. She's crying, not big sobs, but quietly. She opens the closet, seems relieved that her clothes are still there. Grabs an armful in an huge embrace and carries them down to the car. She's back. She goes into our bathroom, takes some stuff from the medicine chest and throws it in her purse. She goes for the hair dryer, discovers it's gone, just shakes her head. She stuffs some bras and panties into her pocketbook; she has to pick them up from the floor. I offer her the money.

56

She looks at it without comprehension. A big green ball the color of lettuce. She shoves it into her pocketbook on top of her panties. She leaves a lot of stuff; I think she'll be back.

★   ★   ★

It's after nine now. The house is cool, from the air conditioning, and pretty much empty, like when we first moved in. I'm sitting on the floor in the kitchen with just the telephone to keep me company. The phone is on the floor too. Its wire is strung across the floor to where I sit with my back against the wall, drinking Coke from a can. The phone actually makes the room look more desolate.

There's a knock at the door. I figure it's Hy. I'm in no mood to get up and answer it. But Hy or whoever knocks again.

When I open the door, it's Miss Lew. She's got my silverware. It's in a tray, and it's wrapped up in cellophane or Saran Wrap or something, and it's got a red bow on it. She hands it to me.

"Thanks," I say. "I'll get you your hundred dollars."

Miss Lew shakes her head. "No. It's a gift. For you and your wife. You have to have something to eat with."

★   ★   ★

I don't know if moments of great shock bring out some buried, essential part of us. Janice got stuck on

"Who are you?" She screamed it over and over. She would have liked to hit me but didn't trust herself. Or, more likely, didn't trust me. Didn't trust that I was sufficiently and familiarly corporeal to take the blow. Maybe she'll send Miss Lew over with her broom. She's going to have a full time job, Miss Lew, scourging our little cul-de-sac.

I believe Janice will be back. A marriage is more than its accumulated possessions. Of course this is about more than the stuff I sold, I realize that. But there's momentum. Our marriage has a certain momentum. It will keep going. I expect we'll sell and move away from Hy and Allison. Okay by me. Janice will miss Miss Lew, though. Not to worry. It's Miami; there are yentas everywhere.

Hy won. He was older, he had more stuff. I explained to him that Janice took the money. He said he didn't care about the money; all he ever wanted was for me to have to run around the cul-de-sac naked. "Boychick, it'll be good for you. I might do it myself." What could I do? I didn't have the money and he wouldn't take it anyway. What could I do? A bet's a bet.

The floor of the bedroom is covered with the contents of the dressers and armoire. A cable wire pokes out of the wall, like a leash without its dog. It's cold, from the air conditioning I had cranked up earlier. I could turn it down, but I would have to get up and go downstairs to do it. Instead I build a nest from the clothes lying around me. I choose Janice's nightgown, fragrant, for my pillow. As I hope to nod off to sleep, I hear a twang from outside. Over and over. It doesn't stop, so I finally get up to look. It's Hy, out in the driveway, bouncing on the trampoline. Naked. Bouncing and bouncing, higher and higher.

The Stove

Fall came. The leaves turned. Daylight savings time ended and it was suddenly dark at 4:30 in the afternoon. When carved pumpkins began to appear on porches, the four of us – Albert, Daemondopolous, Shtarkie, and I – tried to figure out our position on Halloween. We were twelve and too old to put on costumes and go trick-or-treating, although we wouldn't have minded the candy. Billy Mailer, the worst of the Mailer kids, had simplified the trick-or-treat process: he'd wait until some smaller kid had filled a pillowcase, and then he'd mug him for it. Billy had no patience for going door-to-door.

Our social-studies teacher, Miss Trotski, wanted us to trick-or-treat for UNICEF. Daemondopolous tried to explain to her that no adult was going to give money to a bunch of adolescents pretending to be collecting for charity. Even the stupidest adult could see through that. Miss Trotski replied that we'd have little blue-and-silver UNICEF cans, and that she expected adults thought better of us than we thought of ourselves. It was hard not to be in love with Miss Trotski, who never wore a bra and was rumored to be a communist. (Her name didn't help.) So when she gave out the UNICEF cans on Halloween day, we shrugged and took them.

Ours was a neighborhood of two-family homes in upstate New York. My friends and I each lived with our parents on one floor, and a *bubbe* or a *zaide*, or both, lived upstairs. These weren't Norman Rockwell grandparents; these were the sometimes bitter survivors of America's Great Depression and Europe's Holocaust; or, in the case of the Lichts, a personal tragedy.

Like most older neighborhoods, ours had a haunted house. Mrs. Licht and her grown daughter lived in it. (Mr. Licht had died many years earlier.) The lawn was unkempt and overgrown with weeds, the windows had wrought-iron grillwork over them, and the green paint on the clapboards had cracked into a scaly pattern like the skin of a lizard.

Everyone in the neighborhood knew Mrs. Licht's story: during the Depression she had scrimped and saved and had gone without, and she'd kept her dollars hidden away in an old, unused wood stove in the kitchen. (Even a kid, upon hearing this opening line, could guess what happened next.) One day Mrs. Licht's husband came home while she was out shopping, and he lit a fire in the stove. Who knows why. Maybe he was cold. Mrs. Licht came home with her bread and milk and sardines, saw what her husband had done, and went crazy on the spot. She never left the kitchen after that. Day and night, for the rest of her life, she kept a perfect vigil at the stove, as if waiting for some miracle to restore her money. Her husband died. Her two daughters grew up, warped in their own ways by their crazy mother. One moved away, but the other stayed. She worked, she never married, and eventually, so rumor had it, daughter and mother grew well-off. But they went on living as they always had, and Mrs. Licht still wouldn't leave her stove. Her house became the Haunted House, and every child in the neighborhood knew not to go near it. And though my friends and I thought of ourselves as daring in any number of ways, we stayed away too.

Halloween night arrived. The damn UNICEF cans looked at us accusingly. We assumed whatever pennies we could collect would never make it to the big-eyed poster girl, but would be stolen somewhere along the way, because we knew that the Billy Mailers of the world grew up and found more sophisticated ways to plunder trick-or-treaters. But we were restless, and we didn't want to disappoint braless, communist Miss Trotski.

Daemondopolous paid more attention to the world at large than the rest of us did, and in that world there was a Cuban Missile Crisis. So Daemondopolous suggested we put on fake beards and dress up as Fidel

Castro. He thought it would score him some points with Miss Trotski, Fidel being a fellow communist and all. Shtarkie, who was a bit older and could have grown a real beard if they'd let him, seconded the idea. Albert, whose own puberty was nowhere in sight, agreed rather than make an issue of it. I went along with the rest.

We made black beards and green hats from construction paper. When we were done, Daemondopolous looked in the mirror and said "I look like Fidel Douche Bag." But Shtarkie pilfered some real cigars from his dad, and we felt a little better with them stuck in the corners of our mouths. Albert wanted to wear his baseball glove, because he'd heard that Castro had once tried out for the Yankees, but we vetoed the idea. Then we grabbed our little blue-and-silver UNICEF cans and went out.

Everyone thought we were dressed as rabbis. So Rabbi Fidel Castro and Rabbi Raúl Castro and Rabbi Che Guevara and Rabbi Simón Bolívar went house to house for UNICEF, while, ninety miles from Florida, medium-range ballistic missiles threatened to turn Miami into marmalade. People were surprisingly generous. They put dimes and quarters in our cans and gave us candy for ourselves. Emboldened by the warm reception, we stayed out a long time, and when we reconvened at Shtarkie's, our little cans sounded like maracas. We shook them approvingly and fell into the goofy spirit of the night and our costumes and what we called our "redistribution of wealth." Albert revealed that he'd been experimenting with making cider, and that he had a batch fermenting in his basement. We thought we should celebrate, so he went to retrieve his experiment. It tasted like apple juice gone bad, but we drank it anyway, and soon we were back outside singing "What Shall We Do with a Drunken Sailor?" And what began as a guilt-induced but well-intentioned night of charity took a strange turn. We decided to trick-or-treat at the Licht house.

It began with a dare: A while back, Daemondopolous had set himself the goal off taking a dump in the bathroom of every house in the neighborhood. Of course he'd graced Albert's toilet, and Shtarkie's and Billy's and mine. Then he'd begun to knock on doors, feigning an emergency and asking to use the bathroom. It had become a hobby of sorts, like collecting in reverse.

So it was natural, inevitable really, that we dared him to shit in Mrs. Licht's house on Halloween. The mention of Mrs. Licht occasioned one of our rare theological discussions:

"If I were God," Daemondopolous said, "I'd unburn her damn money and put it back in the stove."

The rest of us echoed the sentiment. I think we preferred an activist God to the laissez faire-God whose days of intervention seemed over.

It was Albert who pulled our disparate plans together into one grand scheme: "While Daemondopolous takes a shit in her bathroom, we should put the UNICEF money in her stove."

"How about Daemondopolous takes a shit in the stove?" Shtarkie said.

"Another time," Daemondopolous said.

We put our Fidel hats and beards back on, broke open the UNICEF canisters, and gave the money to Shtarkie in a bag. Then we headed for Mrs. Licht's.

The night was colder now. It was getting late, and most of the trick-or-treaters were home gloating over their spoils. Trudging over the melancholy leaves, I tried to figure out what we'd tell Miss Trotski about the UNICEF cans. It would have been bad enough to return them empty; not to return them at all was going to look terrible. I was further bothered by the fact that we didn't know how much money had burned, and replacing it with thirty-seven dollars and change seemed a decidedly second-class miracle, one that might call into question God's omnipotent nature. Theologically, our plan was flawed from the beginning.

Before I could work through all of my thoughts, though, we arrived at the Licht house. Even Shtarkie and Daemondopolous seemed to hesitate. Albert finally rang the doorbell.

The door opened, and a woman in her forties, the daughter, stood before us in a bathrobe.

"Trick-or-treat."

What else could we say? I think we frightened her as much as she did us. Then she recognized us as neighborhood boys, and her expression changed from frightened to annoyed.

"It's OK if you don't have any candy left," Daemondopolous said. "But could I use your bathroom?"

I think kindness is a natural first reaction to such a request. Daemondopolous looked uncomfortable, and the daughter said OK before a second reaction – a reluctance to let strangers into the house – could set in.

"Where is it?" Daemondopolous asked.

"Can we stand inside? It's cold out," Albert said.

Seeming flustered, the daughter left the door open while she led Daemondopolous to the back of the house. We stood in the vestibule and looked through a living room and a dining room to the kitchen, where, just as the legend had described, a white-haired woman sat before the stove, asleep.

With the daughter gone to take Daemondopolous to the bathroom, Shtarkie slipped out of his moccasins and slipped through the rooms toward the kitchen.

"Where's the light?" we heard Daemondopolous ask, and the daughter went into the bathroom to pull the chain. At that instant, Shtarkie stepped into the kitchen and dropped the bag of coins on the stove. Then he hurried back.

The daughter soon rejoined us in the hall, and we stood in awkward silence for what seemed like an hour. A look of growing consternation crossed the daughter's face.

"What's he doing?" she asked. She must have immediately regretted the question.

Albert paused for a moment, searching for the right word to bridge the gap between this strange adult and us. "BM, I think."

"He couldn't wait until he got home?"

Albert shrugged. And then, to our relief, the toilet flushed, and we heard Daemondopolous washing up. "Thanks," he said to the daughter once he'd returned, and we scrambled out of the house.

We half expected to see a FOR SALE sign on the Licht house the next day, but none appeared. At school we blamed the missing UNICEF cups on Billy Mailer. We could see Miss Trotski wanted to believe us but couldn't.

After school I went to see her alone and told her the truth. (Or most of it. I left out the hard cider and Daemondopolous's dump. I kept the Castro costumes, though, because I thought she'd like that.)

"How could you be so cruel?" she asked. "You have to apologize."

"To UNICEF?" I said. I didn't think my parents would let me go to New York City, to the UN, where I assumed UNICEF lived.

Miss Trotski took a step closer to me and gripped

my shoulders. I tried not to look at the tops of her breasts. "No. To the Lichts."

"Why? We *gave* them money."

"Because you mocked their tragedy."

"We were trying to help them get over it." I believed this.

"No, you weren't. Try to imagine it from their point of view: A woman lives alone with her sick mother. It's dark. It's late. The doorbell rings. She comes to the door and finds four rowdy boys. You won't go away. Later, when she thinks she's rid of you and her ordeal is over, she hears her mother screaming because she's found the money. It was a cruel prank, the cruelest prank you could think of. You need to apologize."

I told her I would. But there were many things I could not do at twelve, and this was one of them. Until then I'd believed that I would be able to do these things when I was grown, and so I'd kept intact my notion of myself as courageous. But I could not imagine ever having the courage to apologize to Mrs. Licht and her daughter. There was no grown-up version of myself that I could picture standing at that door. And I came to think of "grown-up" as a country I would never enter: my visa would forever be denied, and I would be turned away at the border. Oh, sure, Daemondopolous could knock on that door. Hadn't he had taken all those shits in strangers' houses? And Shtarkie, who could already grow a beard, could grow one and stand there, protected by his beard, and do it. And Albert – bright, clueless Albert – could do it, because he wouldn't even understand what he had done. But I couldn't, and I didn't.

I grew up anyway.

Civics Lesson

Why would a middle-aged man, a prosperous middle-aged man, a partner in a architectural firm, the father of two – Sarah 16, Noah 10 – husband in good standing to the lovely Rebecca, a man faithful and considerate (but firm when the occasion warranted), a *macher* in the local conservative synagogue, my long-standing friend and neighbor – why would such a man, a pillar of the community, or at least the embodiment of those pillared qualities, if not a pillar per se – why would such a man, why would this man, Gideon Stern, place on his lawn a chiseled granite statue of two dogs fucking?

The dogs are whippets. The bottom dog wears a look of profound canine indifference while the top dog expectantly sniffs the air, hoping for something better.

I ask Gideon what his wife thinks.

Gideon says: "She's humoring me. Plus she gets sympathy points from all her friends. The only time she lost it was when she heard me telling someone it was her idea."

Gideon and I are on his lawn next to the statue. It's a late spring evening, the grass is green-gold with the setting sun. Behind us shrubs snuggle up to a large white colonial. Two chimneys, like bookends, with the house between them. We are facing the street, watching as passers-by take in the statue.

I ask Gideon what his kids think.

"Sarah loves it. Her friends come by to have their pictures taken with it. Noah's uncomfortable with the attention. He'd like it better if it were on someone else's lawn."

A car slows up. Gideon waves. They speed away.

"Someone you know?"

"No."

I realize, a little too late, that I have been petting the statue, and that this, more than the statue itself, is what caused the car to slow down. I was petting it because it was a dog; and the cool granite just begged to be touched.

Citing the growing coolness of the evening, I say goodnight to Gideon.

★   ★   ★

Gideon's mute on the subject, but I know the ostensible reason for the statue that graces his lawn is this: a high school girl, a friend of Sarah's, has shown up at school with purple hair, has been expelled, and has been championed by a wave of First Amendment letters in the Town Crier, our local rag. Gideon took the girl aside when she was visiting after dinner and told her that her hair looked stupid. "And that's okay. But if you really want to piss your parents off eat lots of red meat and join the Young Republicans. Leave the school out of it; they've got enough trouble without your purple hair."

Shortly after Gideon dispenses his advice, my own daughter, Jessica, returns from softball practice.

"How was practice?"

"Okay. Can you believe they still won't let Stacy back into school? Even after all those people wrote letters."

"I can believe it. I still can't believe she hasn't done the simple thing and colored her hair back."

My daughter is aghast. "What about her First Amendment rights?"

How to explain that First Amendment rights are the least of Stacy's problems. "This isn't about her First Amendment rights." Jessica flops into a chair; she recognizes what she calls my sermon voice and she will hear me out, but she needs to do it sitting down. "Do you think Stacy woke up one morning and said, 'Whoa, I wonder if my First Amendment rights are in working order?' No. This is about Stacy trying to take a short-cut to identity."

"What?"

"This is about Stacy trying to create an identity for herself with hair color."

"I'm going out."

"With David?" David is her sometimes boyfriend.

"With Sarah and some of the other girls on the team. Chicks before dicks."

"What?" I've got to do something about my hearing.

"I'm. Going. Out. With. Sarah." In deference to my hearing problem, my daughter has learned to speak in one-word sentences.

"I thought you said 'Chicks. Before. Dicks.'"

A new tack from Jessica. "Her parents are getting her a lawyer." This is my daughter's trump card.

"I know what's next: 'How come I never get you a lawyer.'" I am pleased with this remark, but my daughter isn't. I'm not taking her seriously. Still I worry sometimes about my daughter's sense of humor.

She gets up from the table and heads toward the stairs. She turns and mouths some words. Just moves her lips, but doesn't say anything. To piss me off. Argue with that.

It's nice, though I don't share this with Jessica's back, to have the luxury to worry about First Amendment issues. I generally worry about receivables – a worry I could eliminate by factoring them at 95% of face, but there go the profits. I worry about John, my youngest – I worry about his eagerness to go along with the crowd. I worry that my hearing is getting worse. I worry about the occasional pain when urinating. I worry about my parents, whose physical failings are more advanced than, and presage, my own.

I worry about my wife. Barb is beginning menopause. I've heard bad things about menopause. I suspect I'm going to be called on for heroic feats of patience and compassion. (Such, no doubt, as my wife routinely performs for me.) I worry that I'm not up to it.

★ ★ ★

"All my friends talk about is menopause." Barb is speaking. The four of us, Rebecca and Gideon, Barb and I, are eating dinner at Cartucci's, salmon colored table clothes and dark green napkins, silverware that thuds if you drop it on the linen tablecloth. A nice place. The table we are seated at is square, and each of us sits opposite the other's spouse. Light, what little of it there is, is provided by the small flame of an oil lamp. The food is good, helped along by the conscious numbing of the other senses.

Barb and Rebecca are comparing notes on menopause, Gideon and I, outsiders to this new and all-consuming new world our wives have entered, are groping for a position peripheral to theirs, something respectful but removed.

There are allegiances here, not just to each other, but to ways of looking at the world, allegiances that may soon be in conflict. Barb and I share a liberal compassion that we hope has grown mellow and tolerant towards life's vicissitudes, but Gideon and I share an ironic detachment to most of what life serves up. In the matter of each other's spouses, Gideon enjoys an easy flirtation with Barb, who likes to be flirted with; but I will not flirt with Rebecca, who doesn't, except that I take her more seriously than Gideon does, a Trojan Horse sort of flirtation that Gideon recognizes and Rebecca doesn't. I am the most gentlemanly of Gideon's friends, Rebecca always says, which – knowing Gideon's other friends – is less of a compliment than it seems. But Rebecca means it to be a compliment.

But the subject is menopause, and Barb is holding forth: "Did you know that Japanese women don't get hot flashes; it's the soy in their diet. They did a study."

Gideon looks up from the menu. "They were hot-flashed for all time at Hiroshima."

All conversations have their subtexts. Gideon is a patriot, fonder of America than is fashionable among the upper middle class. Partly this is his anti-intellectualism; partly it is belonging to a family that came here from an inhospitable Europe.

Nobody wants the next line. Gideon has stopped the menopause conversation, nuked it. A glassy crater like silence settles on the table. The waiter asks if we need another round of drinks. We do.

Rebecca is both lovely and elegant. Her hands, when she does not consciously attend to them, behave as if they were arranging imaginary flowers, and her look, when she doesn't fix you with it, seems to be admiring her handiwork. People remember their manners in her presence.

"To me," Rebecca says, "menopause is like an obnoxious relative at a dinner party, a boor who shows up drunk, disheveled, loud and crude, but who cannot be turned away."

My Barb is more philosophical. "To me," continuing the metaphorical strain, "menopause is part of the great female life cycle" – Gideon has no patience for this outlook, and rolls his eyes to say so; but Barb sticks out her tongue at him and continues – "a dowager aunt, eccentric, intrusive, flighty, petty but somehow an essential member of the family; a desert that defines the oasis."

"For me," Gideon says, "it's the Pied Piper of Hamlin, come to take the children away."

Barb sips her drink and tries to resurrect the conversation: "My friends are all buying soy milk." I think I hear something contemptuous in this remark. Of the soy milk, not her friends.

I say: "I'm sure there will be flavors. Chocolate at least." It occurs to me that menopause is going to be the next great growth industry. "We should buy stock in whoever makes this stuff. In fact – I'm warming to a whole new aspect of this menopause business – we should open The Menopause Store. Get a little kiosk in the Mall. We could call it Victoria's Other Secret. Sell soy milk. Lots of flavors. Calcium supplements.

What else? Books. There must be lots of books about this." I know we won't do this, but someone will. They'll make a fortune. I think I see a faint smile on Barb's face.

★   ★   ★

It's Tuesday, poker night. But Gideon and I are at the Town Hall, in the corridor, waiting for the 7:30 meeting of the Town Planning and Zoning Commission, the TPZ. Fran, the Chairwoman, heads directly for Gideon. She is the size and shape of a fire plug. She is legendary in town for her ability to settle disputes without rancor. She grabs Gideon by a cheek, and pulls his face down to her level. "Gideon. Gideon. What's with these fehcachta dogs? D'Matteo is so excited he got his robe cleaned for this meeting."

"D'Matteo is a putz."

"Yes. Yes. We know this, Gideon. He's a little putz. But this will make him a big putz. He'll run for council on this." Fran still has Gideon by the cheek. Now she pats the other cheek with her free hand. "Take it down. Put it away. Once a year, on Halloween, you bring it out. Okay?"

Gideon removes Fran's hands from his head so he can shake it.

"Gideon. Gideon. A little statue. For the coffee table. That's what you want. A tchatchka. A conversation piece. But small. Proportion, Gideon, proportion."

The meeting is packed with people who don't like dogs. D'Matteo's people. The gist of the TPZ's objection is that the statue is obscene. Gideon expected this, and his response is brief: "What are you going to do, Fran, call a TPZ meeting every time two dogs start sniffing each other's assholes. D'Matteo—"

he lets D'Matteo's name hang there a moment, keeping company with the dogs' assholes – this is an old lawyer's, an old orator's trick – and then continues – "D'Matteo will have to buy another robe."

D'Matteo shoots Gideon a look that says, I think your an asshole too. Fran suggests they get a legal opinion from town council, and adjourns the meeting.

★　★　★

The fact is that Gideon had purchased the statue years ago. He intended it for the cottage he rented each year (and intended to buy) on Otisco Lake. Cottage art tends to be raunchy or in simple bad taste. Black stable boys with Steppin-Fetchit grins, pink flamingos, aw shucks urchins fishing in wishing wells, – well, the dogs would not be out of place. The cottage deal fell through, leaving Gideon's dogs festering in his garage. Among the cottage folk, people whose idea of a compliment was to tell Gideon he wasn't like other Jews – "This from people," Gideon remarked, "more familiar with 'Jew' the verb than 'Jew' the noun" – among these people Gideon's statue would occasion a no more hostile feeling than envy.

★   ★   ★

The Channel 11 Newsmobile pulls up first. A tall white man, at least 6'10", gets out and retrieves a boxy video camera. He pauses to shoot the furry remains of a squirrel flattened against the road.

"Why are you shooting road kill?" I recognize Kim Sung, our buxom Asian news reporter and weekend anchorwoman.

"Just testing."

"Test on the fucking dogs. That's what we're here to cover."

A blue Lincoln pulls up behind the Newsmobile. I hear a pop and watch the trunk open. Then D'Matteo gets out of the car. He's wearing a white, short-sleeved shirt, his forearms covered with curly black hair. He waves at Kim and the camera guy. Then he ducks his head into the trunk. When it comes back out it's wearing a yellow construction hat.

Gideon's daughter Sarah is walking toward the front lawn, aiming a camcorder of her own. Gideon comes out of front door and sits on his front step. Ms. Sung has begun speaking into the microphone. D'Matteo strides purposely toward the statue, holding a sledgehammer by the throat in one hand and a dropcloth in the other.

Gideon thinks about confronting D'Matteo, who is now, technically, trespassing. But D'Matteo has a full head of steam, he has called the news out, he's holding a sledgehammer, which he gives every appearance of knowing how to use. Gideon doesn't think D'Matteo will use it on him; further he judges himself to be stronger than D'Matteo, certainly taller and more fit. And better-looking. That should count for something with the news crew. Still he makes his usual discretion/valor calculation and decides on retaliation. He shouts to D'Matteo, "Come Christmas, your crèche is toast." He resigns his dogs to their fate.

When D'Matteo reaches the statue he looks at Gideon, puts the sledgehammer down and places a foot on it. He then drapes the dropcloth over the statue.

"Cut!" Kim gestures to her camera guy. Then to D'Matteo: "What are you doing?"

D'Matteo is prepared to take his first swing. He turns to Ms. Sung. "What?"

"What are you covering it for?" She remembers to turn off the mike. "I didn't come here to video you sledge-hammering the shit out of a drop cloth." The camera guy and Sarah are getting all this on their camcorders.

"Miss Sung. I can't have chips flying everywhere. What if a piece flies off and puts your pretty eye out. I'm in construction. This is how you do it." He motions her to move back, out of the way. She does, shaking her head. D'Matteo lines up a shot to the higher bump beneath the drop cloth, and then quickly rocks the sledgehammer back and swings it against the statue. The first blow apparently decapitates the male dog. D'Matteo raises both arms, sledgehammer and all, and does a little turn of triumph.

Then he sets about demolishing the rest of the statue. This proves to be hard work. Dark circles spread beneath his arms. His forehead glistens. And soon his initial fury subsides into a steady rhythm, like a convict on a chain gang.

Kim Sung tries to interview Gideon, who replies cryptically, "When your enemy rides in on a donkey, it's enough to remind everyone the donkey's the one on the bottom."

When the show is over, the cameras put away, D'Matteo departed with the head from the statue, Kim comes over to Gideon one more time. "Off the record. Why does a man place a statue of two dogs fucking on his lawn?" I am struck by how eerily this echoes my own question. I think I know the answer, because I know Gideon. Her next question surprises me, but not Gideon. She says, "You weren't born here, were you?"

Gideon smiles. "You weren't either."

"Because I'm Korean? I could have—"

"But you weren't."

Kim nods. Her nod of assent is short, almost imperceptible. I can see that she thinks she understands. Kim has an anchorwoman's perfection. Her hair is long and perfectly black. Her face is without blemish, its features small. She has no accent, and her voice has the pleasant sound of a small bell. She is dressed in a black pants suit, a tight violet sweater beneath it. And yet when our town turns on the nightly news, what they see in their eyes is unmistakably foreign. Kim says, "This isn't about the First Amendment."

It's Gideon's turn to nod. "Nothing is ever about the First Amendment. It's always about something else."

★   ★   ★

Barb and I are eating lunch together. I am squinting at Barb, a shadow haloed by the bright light from the window behind her. I'm not able to search her darkened face for clues. And my hearing is already suspect. She is telling me that Rebecca, that Gideon's wife, had an affair.

"What?" My hearing is suddenly acute, but now my comprehension is suspect. "I can't believe it." Which is true. I don't deny it – how would I know? – but I refuse to believe it. If Rebecca could have an affair, could anyone's wife be trusted? "Who? With who? With whom?"

Barb shakes her head. "Don't know."

"How do you know she had one, then?"

"I do. I know. She's said some things."

"So this is more than just an intuition." I'm hoping that it isn't.

"More than just an intuition." Barb hits the "just" extra hard. We both respect her intuitions.

"Why?"

"Why not?" Barb's teasing me with this. "She just wanted to feel a certain way again?"

"Sleazy?"

"Coveted."

"Does Gideon know?"

"Maybe. He knows something. He knows something is wrong."

"I still can't believe it."

"You're just wishing it was you she was having an affair with." Barb says this mockingly, tenderly.

"I can't believe it." The great challenge of my middle years, so I thought, would be my own fidelity. It never occurred to me that a wife of twenty-five years could be faithless. "Do you feel coveted?"

"Some of the time. Enough."

"Does she get hit on a lot? Rebecca?"

Barb says, "I get hit on a lot."

I measure my response. Incredulity will not be well received and isn't warranted. But I am incredulous. Barb's well known to be married – to me! – and why would anyone hit on her, so clearly unavailable. But she reminds me: her former hairdresser; our son's tennis coach. Those were direct hits; explicit requests for sex. But there were others, ambiguous gestures, that, had I been making them, I would not have trusted my motives. Gifts, ostensibly expressions of gratitude from grateful fathers – Barb's a child psychologist – that were off the mark: too generous, too personal, belonging to the unmistakable category of love offering: roses, chocolates, perfume. So of course the lovely Rebecca gets more than her share, maybe a constant barrage, and in a weak moment, or a brave one – which? – says, "Yes." Meets the look and returns it. Responds not to the innocent surface of some gesture, but to its dark intent.

Barb says she thinks Rebecca initiated it.

Unthinkable!

Seeing my look, Barb offers this consolation: "Maybe she thought Gideon was having an affair and wanted to get even."

"But he wasn't."

"How would you know?" Barb is constantly pointing out to me that we – the men – never talk about anything intimate.

How would I know? I wouldn't. And yet, I know. Gideon is faithful.

I ask, "Will they get divorced?"

"No. I don't think so. The affair is over."

"Do you ever think about Gideon?" I want some conscience-balm for my own lust for Rebecca.

"He's sexy. I don't think about sleeping with him. And it would be no nookie for sure for as long as that statue was on my lawn."

The sunlight, when we leave the restaurant, hits me like a hammer. Barb has sunglasses, and keeps going, but I am momentarily stunned. I squint, but it's not enough; I have to close my eyes for a moment and stand still.

"Are you okay?"

"I'm okay. I just need some sunglasses."

I hear Barb walking back toward me. I open my eyes and force myself to adjust to the sunlight."This is New England. She should wear a scarlet letter."

"This is the twentieth century." Barb takes my arm. "Besides, she has those fucking dogs."

The Hill

"A different god, a different mountain top."
—Chariots of Fire

When you are thirteen, everything fragile is the enemy. So you must break the small windows above the gym, the frail tents the caterpillars weave in the hopes of becoming something better, the thin first skin of ice that forms over the puddles in winter, the thin spirit of the crippled boy.

The crippled boy's name was Reuben. His parents were Holocaust survivors; he was their only child. Our parents arranged for us to play with him. His mother would greet us effusively, as if the visit had been our idea, and our resentment would sour. The chessboard was set up on a tray table in the living room. Around the room the furniture was dark and heavy, furniture, it seemed to me, meant for barring the door against intruders. Like our grandparents, Reuben's mother kept plastic covers on the chairs and sofa. If you sat for the briefest moment, the backs of your legs were soaking wet. There was a dark, sooty patch of wall in one corner, where the Friday night candles were lit. The room held a quiet desolation: no art of course, but no pictures either. A living room that looked like it had been abandoned. There was a small rug under the wooden coffee table, beneath it and everywhere else, a shiny wooden floor. Our houses had wall-to-wall carpeting. (Now of course, I realize the lack of carpeting was on account of the wheel chair.) They never used their fireplace.

Reuben was further separated from us by what his mother called his visions. It wasn't enough that he lived in a wheel chair, that he wore the *pais* and fringes of the orthodox, but he had to have visions. A normal mother would have kept this to herself. A normal boy would have kept it to himself. Our mothers told us of his visions, and we rewarded the news with pained and impatient looks.

Reuben sat there in his wheel chair, in his white birthday shirt, the fringes of his *tallith* hanging down, strange and wrong on every boyhood scale. He would beat us in chess. We would eat some of the bruised fruit or stale pastry his mother brought us. We would leave and swear to ourselves never, ever to come again. He was not friendly or gracious. He liked beating us. But what he really wanted, of course, was to go up The Hill with us. When he asked us we looked away and shrugged: "How?"

The Hill

The fact was that he did not belong on The Hill. You had to climb it under your own power.

The Hill rose to a height slightly higher than the tops of the two story houses adjacent to it. To scale The Hill you scrambled on all fours up the erosion gullies, grabbing bushes and roots for handholds. A six-year-old could climb it and feel like he had accomplished something. The Hill, and hundreds like it, were left during the last ice age, the residue from a receding tongue of ice a mile high and a continent wide. The Hill was an anomaly, the only undeveloped land for miles. Not a park or a nature refuge, it was simply land left over, as the glacier had left it. Among the kids in the neighborhood there was speculation, about who did or didn't own it. No one knew. Anyway, it belonged to us. Even then, it was a mystery that it wasn't developed, that houses hadn't been carved out of it to complete the block. It overlooked the junior high school, its playing field and backstop.

The girls in the neighborhood, mostly our younger sisters – by some flagrant violation of statistical probability we were a neighborhood entirely of older brothers and younger sisters – stayed away from The Hill, singly and as a group. They never went there. They had no interest in it. They never banded together for even the briefest exploration of its possibilities. If it crossed their minds at all, it was as inconceivable a place to visit as the sewer, or the roofs of their own homes. They saw it and ignored it, every day of their lives.

So The Hill was our place. We were alarmed that summer when we saw the trees cobwebbed with the gauze tents of caterpillars. At first we left them alone. We tended to leave things on The Hill alone. Some ecological, some conservative impulse prevailed there that was at odds with the general demeanor of our boyhood. But eventually the tents made us queasy; they made the trees look old and unnatural. In a ritual of purification, we stoned them, stoned every tent the caterpillars made in every crotch of every tree.

When it was my turn to play with Reuben, he shared one of his visions with me. First he beat me quickly at chess. I played poorly on purpose, to spoil his win. I ate a piece of stale pastry. I was ready to leave. He stopped me: "I had a vision about you." It was a plea to stay. I sat down. A smug look came over his face. "It was about your father."

"What about him?" I didn't like this. Our family was off limits to his visions.

He paused. He wanted me to ask. I wanted to leave, so I asked: "What about him? Tell me. You brought it up."

"I had a vision about your father. He was lying down."

I tried to remember if Reuben had ever met my father. I wasn't sure. My father was out of town a lot, on business.

Reuben paused.

"So he was lying down.'"

"Not really lying down. He was lying down dead."

"Where?" Because I needed to invalidate the vision.

"On The Hill."

I felt a surge of relief. Parents never went up on The Hill. Never. Reuben, the poor, dumb, crippled fuck, didn't know this. So his vision, if he had one at all, was suspect.

"My dad never goes up on The Hill. Nobody's parents ever go up on The Hill. Never."

I was shaken though, and I kept an eye on my dad. It didn't do any good. He had two small heart attacks out of town, which he mistook for indigestion, and then a third, a big one that laid him out in the driveway. My mother hustled my sister and I into a bedroom, while the ambulance came and took him to the hospital. They placed him in intensive care. After three days, my mother took my sister and me up to see him. The top part of his bed was encased in an oxygen tent. The sight of the tent made me feel sick and hopeless. But a couple of days later they moved him out of intensive care. And in two weeks he was back home, shaved, and working in his bathrobe at the dining room table.

I decided it was time for Reuben to go up The Hill.

I worked on my best friend, Eric Goldstein – Goldy – after our evening baseball game. Goldy understood the unwritten code of adolescence. We all looked to him for a kind of guidance, and in that he was the uncrowned leader of our group. The sun was almost down, the field was in twilight. The cliffs caught the last of the sun. We weren't quite ready to give up the day; we tossed the hardball back and forth.

I don't think we were bad kids. We obeyed our parents most of the time, certainly to their faces. We were polite to other adults. We went to school, did our homework. We didn't set fires or torture animals. We didn't bully the younger kids. We didn't start fights, but our code of honor required that we not run away from fights that others started. Had Reuben been more likable, we would have treated him better. Had he been a regular boy, in spite of his wheel chair, his orthodoxy, his white shirts, his Holocaust parents, his visions, he could have been one of us. We would have included him. But he was too much the child of his differences. He didn't try hard enough to be like us.

The real business of adolescence is emancipation. Reuben needed a push. He needed to put some distance between his wheel chair and his mother. If we had been bound in a wheel chair, we would have worked out until our arms were as thick as thighs. We would have overcome it. We would have swung around on crutches, like Rosy did when he broke his leg. We would have made something of ourselves. We were disappointed in the way Reuben knuckled under to his paralysis. He needed a kick start. He could be the wheel chair kid who could do fifty chin-ups and an iron cross: that's what we wanted for him. We knew what he needed: less mother, more muscle. He knew it too, at some level. That's why he always brought up The Hill. He just never brought it up the right way. He whined, "Take me up The Hill," like we were his mother, like that was the way it worked.

It was too dark to continue the catch. We sat on the grass. "What about Phil? Will he do it with us?" Goldy was closer to Phil than I was.

Goldy shrugged. Phil Marks was the toughest of us, but also the most afraid of his parents. His father was a small fierce man, aggressively outgoing with adults, and a source of terror to us kids. "If this gets fucked up, his father will kill him."

I didn't see how this could get fucked up, and I said so. "It's not as if he's had a great life 'til now." I continued with my recruiting. "What about Rosy." Steve Rosen might be a problem. He was spending most of his time with Elaine lately.

Goldy understood the issue. Goldy generally defended Rosy to me. He spit. "He'll do it."

"More like he'll say he'll do it," I corrected, "but then he won't show because he's trading tongues with Elaine."

"Do you blame him?"

I shrugged. "Of course not. No. I'm just saying."

We met after school, by the fire escape. Plans were always made at the fire escape that lead from the school gym to the field. Rosy agreed to take the necessary time off from Elaine.

I asked, "Who has to play chess with him next?"

93

Phil grunted.

"OK. You tell him the plan."

There was no plan. We were coming to get him, to take him outside. His mother was thrilled – it was sickening sort of – when all four of us showed up, unbidden, at his door. After much maternal fussing he was launched down the gray wooden ramp from his door to the sidewalk.

When his mother had gone inside – to celebrate with some stale pastry, I imagined – we told him. "We're taking you up The Hill." His hope overcame his normal mistrust of us. He tried to sound indifferent, but his "O.K." was more eager than he intended.

Getting Reuben up The Hill was not easy. We had to take the long route, a long gentle spine that began behind Goldy's garage. We almost never went this way because it wasn't climbing, you didn't have to use your hands. Just a long uphill walk. The sissy route. But carrying Reuben, it was all that we could manage. Besides, it wasn't our test.

Reuben was reluctant to leave his wheel chair. At first, when he grabbed the arms, we thought he was trying to help us by pushing up. But when Goldy and I got our hands under his legs, and began to lift, Reuben still held on. I told him to let go, that we couldn't take the wheel chair up the hill. Carrying him was enough. Reuben let go and grabbed our necks too tightly. He was supposed to casually drape his arms over our shoulders, like the wounded in war movies, glad for the lift but not needy, not desperate. He couldn't get even the simplest things right. I told him to loosen up, we weren't going to drop him.

We made a kind of chair with our arms by grabbing each other's wrists, something we had learned in Cub Scouts. Reuben rested on this bridge. Reuben's mother would have *plotzed* with joy to see him born aloft by his buddies. We followed the narrow path. To the right the cliffs began: a foot or two at first, growing to a full fifteen feet at the top. Goldy was on the cliff side; I was brushing against the sumac bushes on the other. We passed a wild cherry tree; birds and insects always beat us to its fruit. What was left was either rotten or half eaten. Now it was marred by the remnants of the caterpillar tents.

After about twenty yards we switched off. Our wrists stung and our shoulders ached. Although we were doing all the work it was Reuben's sweat I smelled. Phil and Rosy took him the next leg.

When we got to the top we put him down. Somewhat roughly; we were tired. He held himself up in a sitting position, and looked out over the school yard. We were pleased with ourselves, but we didn't know what to do next. We could have talked about girls: who put out, the chances of her putting out for one of us. But we weren't comfortable talking about sex in front of Reuben – we couldn't imagine him ever getting any. One by one the normal topics of our boyhood crossed our minds and were discarded. All contained some affront to what we imagined to be Reuben's feelings. We threw mudballs into the road and watched them disintegrate.

Finally we got bored. It was time to break the news to Reuben. I looked down at the schoolyard where the older boys were playing Flies and Grounders. There was a pause, like a movie out of sync, between the sight of the bat hitting the ball and its sound. Then I looked back at Reuben. He was having a hard time maintaining his contempt for us here where he was at our mercy. I wanted to show him the rest of The Hill, but I didn't want to carry him.

It was quiet. Goldy shot me a glance, which I tried not to notice. This was my idea. I was the master of ceremonies. I had not counted on how thin his useless legs would be, just bones in skin.

It was hopeless. It wasn't that the initiation was a bad idea; he was just too poor a candidate.

Reuben broke the silence. "So what's the big deal? You just come up here to jerk off?" He said this casually, but he looked at me when he was done.

Goldy actually laughed. Reuben, emboldened by Goldy's laughter, went on: "Jerk-off Hill. Jerk-off Hill." He laughed at his own joke, the poor *putz*, and sealed his fate.

I jumped up. I realize now how much I sounded then like the lawyer I was to become. "Look Reuben. You said you wanted us to take you up The Hill. Up (I emphasized the word) The Hill. We've done that.

We've fulfilled our end of the deal. But you never said anything about us taking you back down. Do you understand? You never said anything about us taking you back down." This was positively Talmudic on my part; surely Reuben could appreciate that. "So here's the deal. You have to get down on your own. You can do it." I said this warmly, my voice full of genuine encouragement. "It'll be hard, but you can do it. It'll take guts. You might get a little banged up. But you can do it. The fastest way is over the cliff. You hang first onto the edge, that way it's only about a ten-foot drop. It's caked mud on the bottom, pretty soft landing. It doesn't hurt much, we've all done it." I let that sink in. "Or you can go down the side facing the school yard. You lower yourself by sliding and grabbing onto the roots to slow down. Or you can crawl down the way we came up, but that'll take you forever." This didn't seem like an adequate ending, so I added, "If you do it, we'll take you up here whenever you want." I think I meant that. If not literally, at least in some sense. He could join us. I wasn't sure if we would also take him down in the future; I was still experimenting with the size of my magnanimity.

He was scared. That was OK. We'd all been scared. The issue was: what would he do? If he dragged himself to the cliff and dropped himself off, we could have brought ourselves to like him. It would have been a legendary moment for him, and for us, who brought him to it.

He just sat there. Little by little the fear froze him up.

I said "We're leaving" to prompt some action in him. He said nothing. Having said it, we had no choice. We left. "Don't look back, " I cautioned the others. When we were down The Hill, and looking back up at him, he began to scream.

"*Eema!*" Mother. He screamed it over and over.

It never occurred to us that he would scream for his mother. We would have died on that hill before we would have screamed for our mothers. Had he waited, he could have out-waited us. We would have gone back for him. But he screamed "*Eema*" and we were fucked.

His *eema* came out of the house and looked at us, first in bewilderment and then in horror. Her look of horror was totally out of proportion to what I thought was going on. Goldy said not to worry: we would get him. And we tore up The Hill, up the erosion gullies, scrambling on all fours, indifferent to our own safety, as fast as we could. We brought him down as we had brought him up: the sissy route.

If you think you can imagine the rest, you can't. Not the half of it. We were punished of course. Phil and Rosy, whose bouts of misbehavior were fairly routine, and whose parents were old country in matters of discipline, got the belt. Goldy and I had modern parents. We got lengthy cross-examinations. It came down to this: How could we? We had crossed out of the world of normal adolescent mischief into an outer darkness. There was a lengthy discussion about sending me to a psychologist. No one said it, but Leopold and Loeb were clearly on our parents' minds. In the end our punishment consisted of having lost, irretrievably, some portion of our parents' love and esteem.

We were sent to apologize. To our relief, Reuben's mother did not answer the door. When it became clear that this was a possibility our timid knocks grew louder. Still no answer. Relieved, – you can imagine how little we wanted to face Reuben's mother – we went home.

We were sent back. We were to stay at that door until she answered it.

Finally she did. Her face was wild with hate. She slapped us – hard. Something no parent in our neighborhood ever did to another's child. She tried to spit, not very well or accurately, into my face. "Goyim. You could have killed him." I knew better than to correct her. I apologized. I felt her hate like a sun on my face. And it was over.

He could have made it, and it would have given us something to admire in him. It would have shown some heart, and given him some satisfaction in himself that he was lacking. *Almost killed him?* More like we almost saved his life.

Lake Moriah

"Hunting? You want to go off into the woods and shoot bunny rabbits?" Abe had decided long ago that the easiest way to deny his son something was to ridicule it. Renee, his wife, preferred to simply say "no." They were seated on three sides of a yellow Formica table, worn pale as parchment at the edges. Renee chose to sit facing the lake. On either side they could see the sides of their neighbors' cottages, year-round places, one with a large gray cylinder of propane, the other with a snowmobile crouched under a bright blue tarp.

But Zak persisted: "I would eat whatever I killed."

"And skin it? And gut it?" Abe looked to his wife for support, but Renee declined to comment. Abe watched as she toyed with the squat, candle-filled glass, the yortzeit. Every year Renee lit it in honor of Abe's father. Renee was a convert, and for the most part she practiced her Judaism like an anthropologist, but with the yortzeit she seemed at home. For the memory of her own folks she did nothing. Abe felt enveloped in a bubble of tenderness with her.

Zak broke it. "I would skin it and gut it and cook it and eat it. And clean up afterwards."

Abe looked at the yortzeit, but he asked Zak if he remembered Maury, who was still alive.

"Mr. Klein?" Zak was being treated, now that he was thirteen, to the first names of his father's friends.

Abe nodded. "He got this bug to go hunting. Just when gun control, endangered species, vegetarianism became fashionable."

"Because they became fashionable," Renee amended. Abe knew that what he found pleasantly ironic in Maury, Renee found annoying and immature.

Zak shot his mother an annoyed look. "So?"

"So." Abe shifted forward in his chair, leaning his shoulders into the story, really an anecdote he'd read somewhere that had nothing to do with Maury. "It's deer season. He drives his Lincoln up to the Catskills. The Catskills, for Chrissake. He'll come back with Shecky Green tied to his fender. There haven't been any deer in the Catskills since who knows when. He trudges around in the woods all day long and he doesn't even see a deer. He gets lost. So now he doesn't care about the deer at all, he just wants to find his way back to the Lincoln. And then, like a miracle, there it is: a little cottage, and on its lawn, a deer. Maury can't believe it. He tries to remember what he's supposed to do. Squeeze the trigger. That's the ticket – don't pull the trigger, squeeze it." Abe mimics a trigger slowly being squeezed. "He's like the guy in 'The Tell-Tale Heart,' he raises the rifle so slowly, afraid to make a sound. But when he's ready to shoot, there are these bright mournful eyes." Abe deliberately stopped here, sawed a piece of steak, and started chewing.

"And?"

"He couldn't do it."

Zak made a disgusted stab at his steak. "I could have done it."

"Sure, and you'd have blown the brains out of a plastic lawn ornament." Abe went back to his steak, a sign that this conversation was over.

"If Jews had been hunters, the Nazis wouldn't have had such an easy time killing us." Zak spoke to his plate.

"They fought in Warsaw. Guns aren't much against tanks."

Zak said nothing. He went outside, to the edge of the lake, where he threw stones at an inner tube.

Abe rinsed the dishes. He felt Renee circle her arms around him and rest her cheek against his back. Renee said, "I think what Zak really wants to hunt are Nazis."

★　★　★

In spite of himself, Abe thought about going hunting with Zak, or if not hunting, then white water rafting. Some adventure, with just a hint of danger, to help usher Zak into manhood. Abe thought of Zak as young for his age. Abe was further troubled by the sense he had that other fathers were closer to their sons, spent more time with them, time in which they passed along vast stores of male knowledge pertaining to cars and sports and outdoor life. These of course, but something more essential, the essential loneliness of manhood and self-reliance.

He had mentioned this to Renee once, in the lazy aftermath of their lovemaking. She said, "Teach him to respect women, and he can spend his weekends like you just did, while his buddies are out slapping horseflies in the woods." Renee was a self-described fan of "civilization and its contentments."

Abe often thought of his own father. At thirteen, Max had come to America alone from Russia. Abe had tried to imagine that voyage – the first time when he was a homesick boy of nine at his first overnight camp. Because no details of that crossing were ever provided, Abe supplied his own. A black, four-stack ship, as big as the Titanic, that somehow only sailed at night. In steerage, a word he did not understand but associated with a rat infested cargo hold. A thin boy in tattered knickers and a cap, a Jewish Huck Finn, elated with the adventure of it.

The thought of that voyage dwarfed Abe to this day. Max had a confidence uncluttered by second thoughts. He had decided to come to America at thirteen – thirteen! – and he had done it. Anything was possible for such a man. But his material ambitions had been simple and straightforward. A house, a car, a nice suit. And gadgets: every electronic device sang its siren song to Abe's father. He had the first TV on the block. He had a CB when only truckers had them. He had a car phone before his stockbroker did. He could not pass a video arcade with stopping to play, a short thick water buffalo among a herd of adolescent giraffes. (He would, Abe joked, have traded his stout heart for an infirm one, just to have a pacemaker installed.) It was cancer, a disease without a gadget, that had killed him.

★ ★ ★

Zak was still throwing stones at the inner tube when Abe walked past him, headed for the water. Every day after dinner, when the lake stopped buzzing with water skiers, Abe took his exercise by swimming across. The lake, a reservoir really, was beyond the Catskills, filling a basin between the upstate drumlins. An earth and stone dam pinched off the lake at the south end. Here and there the forest came all the way to the water's edge, obscuring the shoreline.

The metal dock gave a shudder when Abe's first step hit it. There was a fishy smell just at the shoreline. The deck plates were still warm. Abe scratched an itchy instep on the abrasive metal. The end of the dock smelled of tanning oil.

The stone throwing stopped. Renee was coming.

"Abe." He braced himself for the inevitable. "Let me row across with you." The request was too nonchalant.

"No thanks."

"I'll stay out of your way, dear."

"No thank you."

"Then do you mind if I just go for a row? If I see some motorboat heading your way I promise I won't even yell to them."

Zak threw a handful of stones at the tube. Abe walked back to where Renee was standing. He gripped her shoulders in a way that was meant to transmit confidence, but which he quickly realized seemed patronizing. "Allow me this one foolish habit."

"It makes me nervous to watch. They let their kids drive the boats, they get drunk and go for rides."

"Don't watch. Besides they're still at dinner."

Renee creased her brow into a plea. Abe shook his head and walked back to the dock. He heard the cottage door slam.

Zak moved to the dock, testing the water with his feet. "You gonna swim across?"

"Yes."

"Can I come?"

"You're out of shape." This was not strictly true. What was true was that Zak wasn't much of a swimmer. Abe had tried to teach him several times, starting when Zak was six. He no longer had the patience to try.

"I can make it."

"What if you can't?"

"I can make it. If I don't you can save me."

Well, he could. He'd been a lifeguard in high school and college. And they had had this conversation before. "If you get tired we'll head back."

"I won't get tired."

Zak jumped in and started thrashing toward the opposite shore. Abe gave him a head start, then watched, annoyed. He paused to look a moment at the far shore. There was a strip of shadow that would grow thicker as the sun set. When he swam across, Abe was always aware of exactly when he entered the shadow, and when he crossed back out of it on the return lap.

In his college days he had been a distance swimmer, mostly 1500's. He had come to enjoy the trance that came with swimming endless laps. At Zak's age he had already been a strong fluid swimmer, confident in the water. Tonight he went out harder and faster than usual. He wanted to pass Zak up quickly, intimidate him a little, get this charade over. He was 25 yards past Zak when his first burst of energy subsided. He treaded water and waited for Zak to catch up. Then he swam off again, stopped and waited for Zak to catch up. Soon they were half way across.

"I can't swim anymore." Zak's tone was matter-of-fact, as if they were out for a jog, and stopping was a simple matter of plopping down on the curb.

Abe had been waiting for this. He swam back to where his son was struggling.

"Face me. Put your hands on my shoulders. Arms straight. That's right. Keep them straight. Head back. Head back. Legs apart. I'll swim you back." The tired swimmer's carry.

Abe begins a constrained breaststroke, pushing Zak ahead of him. He aims for the opposite shore, judging it to be closer. His stroke is ragged at first. He pulls and kicks harder. It straightens out. Abe wants to speak to Zak, to reassure him – that's part of the process as they teach it in lifesaving classes –, but he can think of nothing to say, and soon he is breathing too hard from the exertion to speak. Tired, he looks across the darkening water to gauge their progress. He sees how far the shore still is, kicks and strokes harder. He monitors his stroke for some flaw, for some reason they have not made greater progress. He concentrates on his hands, presses his fingers into a self-conscious cup, pushes the water back rigidly, with an exaggerated precision, as if he were teaching the stroke. Then he bends his legs in perfect symmetry, gathering them for the kick. And then he kicks. But there is not enough momentum to glide. He strokes again quickly, to keep them above water. He strokes again, desperately, working for the momentary glide in which he will catch his breath. There is no glide and no rest. He strokes again and again, gulping air when he can. The dark water is thicker now, the laws of propulsion are changed. He pulls at the water and it crumbles in his hands. His legs kick in a pile of oily marbles, each kick serves only to rearrange them. He is doing the stroke correctly, with an exaggerated perfection, but there is no movement. He does not dare exhale properly for fear of sinking. The water is cheating him. It has changed. The books all lie, he knows the truth now: people drown because the water changes on them. He has seen a river in winter, a black vein of anthracite coal, a million times more solid than the snow around it. Abe feels a chill spread through him. He gathers strength for one final stroke that will change the water back. He pulls hard with his arms, his skin tensed for signs of betrayal. He whips hard with his legs. He waits for the reassuring sensation of motion, for proof that the water's spell has broken. He waits to glide. But the water slips on the water beneath it and no glide comes. They are drowning.

As a child Abe would pose himself a child's question: if you had a choice and could save yourself or your father, whom would you save? In the full bloom of his innocence he could imagine no harder question. But now they could both drown, or he could save himself. The books all lie: the tragedy is not in the choice, but in the choosing.

"I can swim now." Zak lets go and splashes off as heartily and as awkwardly as at the beginning. Abe turns on his back and floats, forcing his breath into a rhythm. He turns over and takes a few tentative strokes and is pleased to feel the water obey him. He does a slow sidestroke, keeping an eye on Zak. Zak reaches the far shore first and begins to walk back around the lake to their cottage. Abe follows, glad for the distance between them, glad for his rearguard position, glad for the silence, glad even for the penance the mosquitoes exact as he and Zak straggle back through the woods and the yards of strangers.

Getel

I was five or six; we lived in a small village near Grozny. My father was the Rabbi. Rabbi Avrum Ziskoff. We were in his study. I was playing, he was at his books, when the Cossacks flew down into our village and forced their way into the room. They were so tall and big and strange that I thought the room would burst from their noise and abuse. But my father greeted each of them by name, and they grew quiet and obedient, almost like normal men. So I thought, at the time, these are not the Cossacks the old women talk about, who come from nowhere to torment the village.

I did not understand all of my father's conversation. A deal was struck between him and the Cossacks: he would teach them his magic if they would undergo an initiation. In the end, Uncle Azriel, the mohel, was sent for.

I never saw the Cossacks or my father again. My father made me learn two stories, the story of Abraham's covenant with God, and the story of

Abraham's death. He made me repeat them until I had them by heart. Then he pinned a note on me – I still have it – and sent me away. I cried and refused, and he reminded me that he was a Rabbi, that everyone in the village obeyed him, that even these noisy Cossacks obeyed him, that his daughter would obey him, and that no harm would befall me.

The note was on sheepskin, and was repeated in Russian, Yiddish, German, Polish, Hebrew, French, Spanish, Portuguese, Greek, Latin, and Arabic. The note said, "My name is Getel. My father is Rabbi Avrum Ziskoff, a servant of the God of Moses." My father knew English too, of course, but there was no English on the note. His notion was that the authorities would stop me only when they no longer understood the note, and my destination was America.

Much later, when I had travelled so long that my clothes no longer fit me properly, I was stopped by a uniformed man who could not read my note. He called another uniformed man over, and then another, until a swarm of uniformed and uncomprehending men surrounded me. None of them understood the note, so I expected I was in America and would go no farther.

At the end of the quarantine, a man who dressed and carried himself like my father came and got me. He spoke to the authorities in English, and to me in Russian. He said, "I am Rabbi Joseph Solomon. Welcome to New York." He wanted to unpin the note, but I wouldn't let him. I struggled and because I didn't want to cry I blurted out the two stories my father had made me memorize. Rabbi Solomon whistled, and spoke in English to no one in particular. My father had this habit, so I was put at ease. He left the note alone. I told him about the Cossacks, how my father had made them quiet, how he had sent for Uncle Azreiel, how I had been sent away. This new Rabbi just whistled, and talked out loud again to no one in particular.

He took me to his home, and I met his wife and daughter. Yetta was about my age at the time and spoiled. So I was bragging to her about my father. I said he knew everyone's name, even people he had never met. Yetta called me liar; she said no one could know everyone's name. I said God could, and my father could. Yetta's father came in to settle the fight, and when it was my turn I stood my ground, and blurted out every Cossack's name – every Dmitri, Fyodor, Mikhail, Alyosha, Illya – every one of them, just as my father had on the afternoon when I had last seen him.

At that point Yetta's father took her aside and explained, loud enough for me to hear, that with God, anything is possible. Yetta became quiet at this, and so did I. Even Yetta's father became quiet, and looked, wrapped in his silence, like the Cossacks after my father had called them by name.

That afternoon passed like a dream, with everyone tiptoeing around me; and when they did speak to me the words were like words in a dream, passing directly from their mouths to my brain. I couldn't remember hearing the sound of them being spoken. That evening, as I lay in bed, I heard the sounds of visitors. Yetta's father got me out of bed, and told me to get dressed. I put on my clothes in the darkness, and waited. Yetta's father brought me downstairs to his study, where other men, rabbis, argued until they noticed me, and then they fell silent. Rabbi Solomon spoke: "Do you remember everything you said to me when I first came for you?" I nodded. "Could you tell me again?" Rabbi Solomon was speaking in Russian, and he made no mention of the others around him.

I hesitated and then spoke, also in Russian, afraid that if I got one word wrong something terrible would happen to me. I saw one of the others whispering, and that made me even more afraid until Rabbi Solomon said simply, "He's translating."

So I told them again about the Cossacks, how they wanted to learn my father's trick of knowing their names, how he sent for the mohel, how he taught me the story of Abraham and the circumcision of all his household, even the servants, and the story of Abraham's death. No one spoke, and their silence seemed to suck all the air from the room so that I had to breathe deeper and deeper, and my eyes were sore from meeting so many stares so that soon they were filled with tears and I was sobbing. Then I knew I was crying not for the silence or the stares, but for the story, because I read its meaning in the faces of the others.

They took off my shoes, put slippers on my feet, and said the Kaddish, the prayer for the dead.

About the Author

Howard Luxenberg grew up in Syracuse, New York. Short fiction of his has appeared in *Tin House, The Iowa Review, The Sun, The Gettysburg Review, Alaska Quarterly Review,* and *Other Voices* and has been included in the anthology *Best of Tin House*. His thriller, *Mayan Star*, appears under his pen name, Howard Allan.

Made in the USA
Lexington, KY
10 August 2019